100 New Zealand
Short Short Stories 4

100 New Zealand Short Short Stories 4

edited by Stephen Stratford

TANDEM PRESS

First published in New Zealand in 2000 by
Tandem Press
2 Rugby Road
Birkenhead, Auckland
New Zealand

ISBN 1 877178 71 3

The publishers gratefully acknowledge the assistance of
Creative NZ in the production of this book.

Cover and text design: Jacinda Torrance, Verso Design
Text editor: Jeanette Cook
Production: BookNZ
Printed in New Zealand by Publishing Press

contents

9   *Acknowledgements*

10   *Introduction*

13   **This Is How Good the Coffee Is** • *Denise Sammons*

14   **Burgeoning** • *Rhonda Bartle*

16   **Four Fish** • *James Norcliffe*

18   **Nurture** • *Graeme Lay*

20   **The Tissue Seller** • *Kapka Kassabova*

22   **Birds of Feathers** • *Kevin Ireland*

25   **The Lepidopterist and the Waterlily** • *Judy Parker*

26   **Night Watchman** • *Judith White*

28   **Cold** • *Jackie Davis*

30   **When You Go to San Francisco Be Sure to Wear Flowers in Your Hair** • *Margaret Crawford*

32   **Queen of the Snows** • *Tim Jones*

34   **Learning Greek** • *Adrienne Rewi*

36   **Visiting Rights** • *Bridget Musters*

38   **Sunday at the Beach with George** • *Isa Moynihan*

40   **Nor'wester** • *Tracey Edginton*

42   **Departure** • *Stephen Stratford*

44   **Falling** • *Diane Brown*

46   **'True Facts About Girls Who Smoke and Drink Liquor'** • *Jane Bissell*

48   **Step Forward, Step Back** • *Sarah Quigley*

50   **Eve and Adam** • *Bernard Steeds*

52   **Spain-ish Hearts** • *Katy Dugdale*

54   **The Sack Man** • *Michael Bland*

56   **The Flat Rock Club** • *Jon Thomas*

58   **Their House Up North** • *Jane Blaikie*

60   **Expunging God** • *Bronwyn Tate*

62   **The Lighthouse** • *Grant Dale*

64   **The Lives of Bryan** • *John McCrystal*

66   **Going to Town** • *Victoria Cleal*

68   **To Hide the Hook** • *Garry P Sommerville*

70   **Dahlias** • *Doug Coutts*

72   **Postcard** • *Rachel Buchanan*

74   **Sparklers** • *Tamzin Blair*

76   **Good for a Laugh** • *Trudi Cameron*

78   **Emily's Dahlias** • *Catherine Mair*

80   **Man Alone** • *Jerry Chunn*

82   **Dramatis Personae** • *Janette Sinclair*

84   **He Lies Down** • *Geoff Allen*

86   **Queen of the Night** • *Penelope Bieder*

88   **Cynthia's Landmine Blue** • *Katie Henderson*

90   **Bernie's Bird Trick** • *Frank Nerney*

92   **The Truckie** • *Maureen Langford*

95   **Beyond** • *Peter Bland*

97   **Ruby Anniversary** • *Bernard Brown*

98   **The Key** • *John Allison*

100   **Diamonds are Green** • *Laurie Mantell*

102   **The Panda Family** • *Jan Marsh*

104   **That Summer, the Longing Summer** • *Kiyohiro Ejima*

106   **The Butterfly Orchid** • *Virginia Fenton*

108 **Away with Words** • *David Hill*

110 **Wai** • *Phil Kawana*

112 **Equality** • *Kathryn Simmonds*

114 **Mickey** • *Janis Freegard*

116 **Vintage** • *Geoff Henshaw*

118 **The Greenest Car in New Zealand** • *Frank Fell*

119 **Lunch** • *Adrienne Koreman*

120 **Airport** • *Vivienne Shakespear*

122 **Spa** • *Sarah Weir*

124 **Walking Backwards** • *Patricia Lawson*

126 **Ghouls Will Be Ghouls** • *Linda Burgess*

128 **Yes or No** • *Lisette de Jong*

130 **Inner-City Room To Let** • *Bill Payne*

132 **Anzac** • *Elisabeth Liebert*

134 **A Gothic Folly** • *David Eggleton*

136 **The Thief's Journal** • *David Lyndon Brown*

138 **Now You See Me. Now You Don't.** • *Jo White*

140 **Gwen's 90th** • *Linda Gill*

142 **Now This** • *Simon Reeve*

144 **Parting Shots** • *Alastair Agnew*

146 **Moment of Truth** • *Jane Riley*

148 **Sleepwalking over the Bumps** • *Gerry Webb*

150 **Keeping up with Hermione** • *Helen Mulgan*

152 **A Slight Change in the Weather** • *Raewyn Alexander*

154 **Swans on the Water** • *Phillip Wilson*

156 **Aunt Sylvia's Silver** • *Joy MacKenzie*

158 **Rosalie, RIP** • *Sheridan Keith*

160 **Child's Play** • *Ro Cambridge*

162 **The Epiphany of Sister Patrice** • *Frankie McMillan*

164 **The Daisy Patch** • *Jeanette Galpin*

166 **He Drove a Yellow Cortina** • *Jackie Mason*

168 **Memories** • *Dorothy Black*

170 **Morning** • *Idoya Munn*

172 **Fanny's Stories** • *Jan Farr*

174 **Brain** • *Victoria Frame*

176 **Balls of Steel** • *Karen Tay*

178 **More Turtles** • *Ross Lay*

180 **It Has No Name** • *Dena Thorne-Pezet*

182 **Eleven-Eight Time** • *Suzanne Gee*

184 **Morning, Noon and Night** • *Rowan Miller*

186 **War Games** • *Janet Tyler*

188 **Snow** • *Heather Snow*

190 **Come Home Chrome Dome** • *Lesley Wallis*

192 **The Carp** • *Richard von Sturmer*

194 **Growth** • *Louise Wrightson*

196 **The Gardenia Tree** • *Kellyana Morey*

198 **Magic** • *Pip Robertson*

200 **Crown Lynn** • *Cherie Barford*

202 **Jonah at Kapiti** • *Bill Direen*

204 **China Doll** • *Andrew M Bell*

206 **A Matter of Taste** • *Claire Beynon*

208 **Silver Bullet: The Dorm Version** • *Michael Laws*

210 **Competition finalists**

211 **Notes on contributors**

acknowledgements

The editor and publisher would like to thank Graeme Lay for his invaluable expertise, Sarah Fraser for her patience and Rachel Clare for her word-processing skills.

introduction

As with the second and third volumes in this series, a competition was held to attract submissions. The initial competition drew 800 entries, and for *The Third Century* there were 920. This time there were 1273 entries, well over half a million words and an increase of 38 percent over the previous year. This productivity gain must be the envy of every other industry.

The entries came from all over the country, with strong showings from places like Takaka and Oamaru – though Oamaru is a famous producer of literary talent (Frame, Marshall, McGee), so perhaps that shouldn't be a surprise. Entries also came from Taiwan, Thailand, England, Australia, Holland, the Gulf States and other countries where New Zealanders, in time-honoured fashion, are pursuing their overseas experience. Some entrants were still at school; the youngest selected was born in 1981 and the oldest in 1913. Ethnicity includes Pakeha, Maori, Samoan, Rotuman, Chinese, Japanese and Bulgarian. There are several scientists, a few poets, a doctor, a psychologist, an accountant, a photographer, a former MP and an impressive number of full-time writers.

The short short story is a difficult form. To write a good one is much harder than it looks and requires a poet's concentration of thought, image and language. In the most successful examples, every word works hard to justify its position, contributing to the three basic building blocks of plot, characterisation and setting. The language in these stories is also used in a fresh way: not straining for effect but quietly surprising the reader with images that are as apt as they are unexpected. At its best, the short short story is a slight-seeming piece that in fact contains a world of thought and feeling, and is all the more effective for giving the reader so much in such a concentrated burst. It offers bite-sized pleasure and delight, and as much sustenance as its bigger siblings.

Not all the 1273 entries were of this standard. Many were simple yarns told in the plainest of plain English. Many more were in the venerable O Henry tradition with a (usually predictable) twist in the tale: I wouldn't mind a dollar for every one that revealed the narrator to be a cat or dog. Then there were the revenge fantasies: a vaguely disturbing number of stories by women concerned a female character's desire to murder or at least take physical revenge on her husband. Few men wrote such stories about disposing of their wives, which may or may not tell us something about the state of marriage in New Zealand.

Other popular topics were old people in rest homes; child abuse in its various forms; the effects of poverty; children in broken families; the difficulty of being a teenager, and of being a writer. Some of these were excellent, but in proportion to their number few were selected for publication. This was for two reasons. First, these writers paid less attention to their use of language than to conveying the dreariness and despair of their characters' lives, so the writing was often as drab as the subject matter. Second, editorial fatigue sets in: one can take only so much darkness, and a slight bias to the quirky and entertaining is inevitable.

Twelve finalists were selected to pass on to this year's Tandem Press Short Short Story Competition judge, novelist and short story writer Shonagh Koea. She said of the winning story, Denise Sammons's 'This Is How Good the Coffee Is', that its 'literary ethos and naturalism give an emotional plausibility to an isolated character in a tiny, but defining, personal moment of realisation and identification. To this minuscule story, faint as the mark of a seabird's claw on wet sand, I give first place because in twenty-one short lines on A4 paper there is suddenly the skeletal scenario of loss, betrayal, imagined revival, equally imagined defeat and terror of loneliness, outlined in a few clear strokes.'

Of the runner-up, Rhonda Bartle's 'Burgeoning', the judge said that 'in a very small space it is a vivid and fascinating literary achievement in manners and emotional stance'. Third-placed was James Norcliffe's 'Four Fish', of which the judge said that the boy and his uncle 'have an attitude to their activities that is at once perverse and horrible, outlined in this tiny and merciless tale with a few deft strokes'.

Shonagh Koea also singled out Maureen Langford's 'The Truckie', Jane Bissell's 'True facts About Girls Who Smoke and Drink Liquor' and Virginia Fenton's 'The Butterfly Orchid'. These and the other ninety-four stories in this collection make as varied a set of stories, styles and voices as one could find between the covers of one book.

Stephen Stratford

This Is How Good the Coffee Is

Denise Sammons

It's a grey day, raining and cold, yet I'm sitting, under shelter, outside. Happy. I am loving the feeling of a clamouring stopping. Then a tram full of American tourists pulls up outside the café and empties its cargo onto the footpath. A woman dressed in pink is telling another – who looks like a basketball on legs, all round and striped – about her problem. 'Oh,' her friend says, 'there's a product on the market for that.'

I sit in the noise and feel a kindness, a warmth, maybe even some kind of love for these loud people. This is how good the coffee is.

I am thinking of the French doors at home and how they will be leaking now (don't tell the real estate agent). Or do tell the real estate agent and maybe our house will never sell. Yes. I am imagining the soft plop, plop of the drops on the inside of the glass. I know you are at home with the open-mouthed boxes that are waiting to swallow our life together. You will be sitting with the cats, reassuring the ones you are taking and saying goodbye to the ones staying with me. In this moment I can almost see how it could all work out for the best. This is how good the coffee is.

Sparrows ring the table where I am sitting. They skid towards my plate, aiming for the muffin, but then they get frightened and slide back to the edge of the table. They have no staying power. Their claws have no traction. Up close their bland commonness is transformed into beauty. The striking marking on their wings making a pleasing contrast to the soft, downy bodies. I want to hold one in my hand so some of that softness could seep into me, into my heart. I know that's impossible. I think of her. I do not smile. No coffee is that good.

Burgeoning

Rhonda Bartle

They buy a house in the country, a two-storied dilapidated affair that wears a veranda like britches dropped around its ankles. They stand at the gate at the end of the drive. The track is full of holes. The van is full of everything they own – one fridge, three chrome chairs, one table painted white, a bed. A dale of tea towels, dishes, spoons. A hill of love letters.

'What do you think?' he asks.

'It's big,' she says. 'Bigger than I thought.'

'Yup,' he agrees. The first mortgage payment is due at the end of the month. 'She's big all right.'

'It's going to be very draughty in autumn,' she says.

She's watching tattered curtains being sucked over sills upstairs. Downstairs, they don't exist.

'I'll fix the windows up,' he says. 'We'll use coloured glass.'

'Take a bit to keep it warm in winter,' she says. 'Take a bit to heat.'

'Still, plenty of wood,' he says.

He swivels round, points out distant trees that look as though they all died at once. A mess of amputated arms and legs. A thicket.

'Come in very handy, those,' he says.

'I bet the roof leaks,' she sighs.

'Old roofs always leak,' he says. 'Especially when it rains.'

He smiles in her direction but she's not looking.

'It's going to be hot in summer,' she says. 'Not much shade.'

She's right. There's no shade anywhere. Apart from the dead trees there's not a stick of orchard, a blade of lawn. The house sits on its own shadow and that's all there is.

'I'll fix the porch,' he says. 'I'll fix it so well you'd never know how bad it was to start with. We'll put the chairs out there.'

The late sun drops through the slats missing overhead and makes a pattern like a keyboard on the ground. He has the absurd desire to step out a tune on the light and dark fingers.

'It'll be perfect in spring,' he says. 'Not too hot, not too cold. It'll be just right.' He knows he sounds like Goldilocks but he doesn't care. He's watching her face. He's waiting. Starlings swim through the fading warmth up to the roofline where some sit sentry on the smokestack. Others disappear under the eaves. They're building nests.

'It's too early in the season, really,' she says with a small frown. She leans a cheek against his.

'I'll plant some trees,' she says at last. 'For the birds.'

Four Fish

James Norcliffe

The first fish

was a kahawai. 'Great fish,' said Uncle Gordon. 'They fight like bastards.'

This one did. Uncle Gordon ran down the sandy slope of the beach and flung his surfcaster over his broad shoulder. The heavy spoon whistled high and unbelievably far, far beyond the breaking waves, the nylon line billowing in its wake. There was a barely perceptible splash of white, then Uncle Gordon reeled in furiously so that the silver spoon came jinking back towards him like a terrified herring.

My own efforts were pitiful so I gave them up to admire him. Quite soon he hooked a kahawai and, sure enough, it fought like a bastard. Uncle Gordon played it with finesse. The rod strained and bent double as he pulled it in, then straightened again as he let it run, the reel whirring. When finally the huge kahawai was flopping exhausted in the ripples he let me net it and bring it to him.

Almost the first thing he did was lift it by the tail, bring it over his head, and thwack it on the hard wet sand half a dozen times.

'Dry as a bastard if you don't do that,' he grunted.

The second fish

was a blind eel. We were on the jetty and there was a commotion. People pointing, shouting in disgust. On the blue surface a blind eel was lazily swimming. It looked disgusting: a wobbly grey surrounded by a miasma of pinkish mucus. Uncle Gordon put it best: a great dick swimming in its own spunk, he said. Then he sent me to get some stones so he could pelt it savagely.

'If that bastard stuff gets on your line you'll never catch another fish,' he said.

The third fish

was a butterfish. They were hard to catch as they lurked in the bull kelp. When he caught one, Uncle Gordon took his knife and sliced the struggling fish in two. He tugged at the guts and flicked them into the pool; then he peeled back the fillet to show me the pattern of fine green bones.

'Beautiful,' he said. 'Green bone. Sweet as a bastard to eat, these things.'

The fourth fish

Uncle Gordon took me into the Adelphi.

'Give the boy a beer, Helen,' he said. 'He's just about old enough. And have something yourself.'

'You paying, Gordy?'

Uncle Gordon nodded.

'In that case I might just have myself an Eskimo Nell.'

Helen took a glass large enough to be a small vase and filled it from a succession of bottles: green stuff, gold stuff, white stuff. When she'd finished, the layers in the vase made it look like a rugby sock. 'Cheers,' she said.

Uncle Gordon stared at her, then he led me to a table by the window. After pouring himself a beer, he looked back at Helen who raised her huge glass at him in salute.

'Helen can be a funny bastard sometimes,' he said. 'Have another?'

Nurture

Graeme Lay

'Bonjour, chérie!'

Even by the usual transvestite standards, young Joel was outrageous. Every day as he served Tiare and me our hotel meals, he flounced, whirled and crooned Tahitian songs. Tall, dark-skinned and with fine, regular features, he waltzed rather than walked about the dining room. Placing a sliced baguette and jam in front of us, Joel flashed his ebony eyes at Tiare. This morning his head was crowned with a garland of tiny, multicoloured flowers. He only glanced at me before pirouetting back into the kitchen on his long bare feet. Tiare smiled slyly.

'He fancies you.'

'Good God, why do you say that?'

'A woman always knows.'

She dissolved into giggles, clearly enjoying my discomfort. I was struck by the way her body language resembled Joel's. Curious about the men-women, I said, 'Is it true that the transvestites here are created by their parents? That if a couple doesn't have a daughter they treat one of their sons as a girl, so that they grow up female?'

Tiare shook her head firmly. 'It's *not true*. No parent would do such a thing. Can you imagine me putting one of my boys in a dress?'

I laughed. Tiare had five strapping sons, aged between thirteen and eighteen. The thought of any of them in drag was absurd. 'So it's just another South Pacific myth?'

'Yes. It happens because it's in their genes.' She looked challenging. 'And here they're not repressed, like in your part of the world, so they're not ashamed of behaving openly like women.'

I nodded. I didn't want an argument. We had a long day's touring ahead of us. As we left the hotel, Joel blew an extravagant kiss to her, rippled his fingers at me. 'Bonne journée, mes chères!' he called.

Deep in the Taipivai valley, Tiare pulled the jeep to the roadside. The house was scarcely visible, so crowded with tropical foliage was its section. In the house was the workshop of the best wood carver on Nuku Hiva, she had told me. We made our way through the luxuriant foliage. Then, at the front door of the house, we stopped.

Sitting on the step, smiling up at us, was the most beautiful child I had ever seen. She had huge brown eyes and long black curls. Her beige skin was flawless, her lashes long, her cupid mouth was a delicate pink, the same shade as her frilly, floral-patterned dress. She looked about five. Quite smitten, I bowed and held my hand out to her.

'Bonjour mam'selle!' I declared.

The child produced a torrent of delighted giggles. But instead of taking my hand she stood up, and in one sweeping movement hoisted her dress high over her head. Our eyes went straight to the bare round belly, the button navel, the tightly balled scrotum, the hanging, pointed penis.

Tiare's stunned gaze moved to me, reflecting my own. Through the cotton of the still-uplifted dress, the child was still laughing.

The Tissue Seller

Kapka Kassabova

He had green eyes and Bollywood looks. But he was not in Bollywood – he was a tissue-seller at the fifth traffic-lights on a busy Bombay road. He balanced a vertiginous stack of cardboard tissue-boxes in pastel shades with *Western* written over them in bold, hopeful letters. He wriggled his way across the five lanes, his stack lurching towards open car windows inside which the indifferent sat. The indifferent, the tight-fisted, the contemptuous, the tissue-immune. Their boredom was his hope. He existed between red lights. He wished he could move at the speed with which the afternoon heat crushed him.

When he saw the white memsahib in the shiny jeep, he hurried towards her, squirming among the steel bodies of the indifferent, the tight-fisted, the contemptuous, the tissue-immune. The lights would soon turn green and today's first and last chance would be lost. The jeep was first in the line.

The memsahib sat placidly in the back seat while her driver wiped his forehead with a handkerchief. 'Madam!' he cried, 'Madam, twenty rupees!' The driver shooed him away. The top box fell off. 'Madam!' He freed one hand to knock on her window. She looked at him with eyes in which hesitation glimmered. 'Fifteen rupees,' he cried. He pressed his face to her window. Another box fell off but he couldn't risk bending down to pick it up. She took out some notes and reached towards her driver.

Then suddenly, they were off. The hateful green light mocked his despair. The monster of traffic moved forward.

He ran. The jeep was moving so slowly that he could almost keep up the same level as the white face, which looked at him in surprise.

'Madam!' he screamed above the thousand engines. At first he held the boxes with both arms but soon had to give up his left arm in order to move faster. Three more boxes fell off. Horns chased him in an increasing crescendo, but he could scream louder. 'Madam!' He could not afford to lose the silver jeep from sight, even if it was getting smaller and smaller in the flood of traffic. He ran at the speed with which the heat denied movement. He ran for today's first and last chance. He ran and thought of his boxes crushed by tyres in his wake, lost forever. He had to sell these two, there was no choice.

And then the miracle happened. The jeep changed lanes, moved to the left and pulled over. He zipped across the five lanes, the flash of his body cutting through steel, smoke and glass. Nothing could touch him now.

By the time he reached her window again, he had no breath left but he didn't need his breath any more. The memsahib wound her window down and handed him fifty rupees. Fifty! He tumbled the two boxes into her lap and clutched the note in his wet hand. 'Thank you, Madam,' he whispered with the parched desert that was his mouth. Her thin lips smiled.

In a delirium of heat and happiness, he waved to her. Perhaps she waved back. He didn't see, because a truck thundered behind him, through him, over him, at the exact speed at which the afternoon heat made the memsahib in the jeep weep with nervous exhaustion and reach for a tissue.

Birds of Feathers

Kevin Ireland

It was almost impossible that my brother Jim's wife's half-sister's uncle-by-marriage could have been a blood relation, a blessing for which I once felt truly thankful.

His name was Fred Feathers and his main claim to fame was that forty years ago he was apprehended by the police in broad daylight, racing up Queen Street in women's clothing. The details appeared in *Truth*, and the scandal meant our family cut him completely – except for my sister Sue and her husband Harry.

They've always been soft, so I wasn't surprised to hear later that they kept in touch. I imagined they discussed the latest frocks in *Vogue*.

I saw Fred's death notice ages ago, and I suppose I wished him 'Good riddance' – until last October, when Sue and Harry asked me around to meet a lawyer and I was stunned to learn that, through legal arrangements and a sequence of deaths, we three had become the beneficiaries of Fred Feathers's considerable estate.

Imagine how I felt. I'd always detested the man. 'Count me out. I'm not having any,' I told Harry, after the lawyer had gone.

'Don't be so bloody judgmental. You wouldn't have a dollar in your pocket if you could find out where it'd been,' Harry joked.

'That's not funny,' I insisted. 'I'm talking principles.'

'Well then, you'd better listen to your sister,' he argued.

Harry poured a drink, and the next shock of the day was when Sue explained about Fred. Apparently he'd been in bed in a Queen Street hotel, with an unnamed member of our family, when some snoop tried breaking in, and Fred, whose trousers were in the bathroom, pulled on the woman's dress, then scrambled down the fire escape and hared off, only to get stopped by the police.

'He was a gentleman,' Sue insisted. 'He took his medicine in order to protect the reputation of someone near and dear to us.'

There was a silence, then Harry refilled our glasses.

'Was it you?' I asked quietly. Sue would have just about been the legal age.

'Don't be stupid,' she said.

I began to sweat. 'That leaves Jim's wife, her half-sister, aunt Beth, my ex-wife, and who else?'

'I'm not saying,' Sue said definitely.

'Christ, not Mum?' I whispered.

'My lips are sealed.'

There was another long silence, then Harry filled my glass right to the top and suggested, 'You could use the money to do good works.'

'Why wasn't I told long ago?' I demanded.

'The scandal would've killed Whoever,' Sue explained.

I took a taxi home, after promising that I'd think over the bequest after all.

That was months ago, and naturally I gave in. But I've never touched my share, and I still can't go near it. It's as though there's a contagion of suspicion infecting me.

Harry was right. It's not the money that seems contaminated. But a whole lot of cherished memories have been twisted and polluted forever.

The worst of them is the haunting image of Fred dashing through the middle of town in a dress I would have previously seen on one of only six women in my family circle.

I once used to sneer at Fred. I used to refer to him as a deviant, and I often called people like him 'birds of Feathers'. But I now think of him as far more colourful and audacious and exotic than that. Sometimes I dream what it would be like to have the comic bravery to spread my wings as he did. But the truth is, I'd sacrifice his nest egg just to be able to laugh.

The Lepidopterist and the Waterlily

Judy Parker

There is a lepidopterist and a waterlily.

The lepidopterist has a net in his hand.

The waterlily has a *Papilio ulysses* resting on one of its leaves. It has come to investigate a blue lure that has been set at the water's edge.

Just as the lepidopterist raises his net to capture his prize, the waterlily sends up a new shoot, and when the bud begins to open, instead of petals, a tiny wall unfolds. A tiny terracotta wall with moss in its crevices.

With his net transfixed in the air, the lepidopterist watches the tiny wall bloom larger and larger. The butterfly, startled, flies a little way up the wall landing just out of reach, so the lepidopterist must put his foot in a crack and climb a little to catch it.

Once more it flies out of reach, so the lepidopterist puts his net between his teeth, and scrambles with bleeding fingers a little further and a little further after his *ulysses*, till he has climbed all the way up to the top. He looks over.

From the top of his wall to the horizon, in every direction, is an intricate network of walls, being scaled by identical men, and above the head of each a single *ulysses*, there in that instant of torment before it is caught.

Night Watchman

Judith White

Come in, she says to him, accepting the flowers and the flickering kiss on her cheek.

From my room next door, I spy silhouettes – shadow puppets dancing on the curtains. Her face is tilted towards his. I see his hand behind her neck, untying the tight knot to allow a cascading of hair upon her shoulders. He and she merge into one, an unmoving statue in an enchanted room.

The night is thick with heat, crickets beating their shrill but dull monotone. My own breath is barely stirring, my heart's pale throb echoing distant drums, the pulse of ancient music, of primitive ceremonies and rituals …

A bird shrieks and I realise the window is empty, the curtains once more a blank screen of folds and shadows.

The next morning I see her sitting on the top step of her porch, her full skirt tucked around her tanned bare legs. Sewing. Hemming around the edges of a velvet black cloak, the endless horizon of a night sky. She lifts her eyes to mine, defiantly. The prick of the needle pierces my sick heart.

Later, mats are shaken, dust rises. I hear the swish of a broom, the foamy slop and slosh of a mop. Then I hear the running of bath water, smell steamy perfume drifting across the afternoon.

The air crackles with heat.

My mouth like pumice.

A ruffle of shadows edges the day along, towards evening.

She appears at dusk in a red dress with the cloak hanging from her shoulders. She lights a candle and places it between two glasses and a bottle of champagne on the garden table.

I hear the rumble of his car, the footsteps down the driveway. He's wearing a suit, pulling at the sleeves beneath his jacket, tugging at his tie. She's laughing as she studies him, pecks at fluff on his shoulder, summons him to be seated. He crosses and uncrosses his leg, shifts in his seat, crosses the other leg. Pats his jacket pocket. Scratches his cheek.

She pours champagne, still beaming at him; he responds with a nervous smile.

Out in the streets, a bus throbs like an old dog.

The air, motionless, suddenly chills. She stands up, her arms outstretched, the cloak billowing like the wings of a huge bat. She wraps her arms around him, and he, unresisting, is swallowed by the cloak. Sucked like a genie into a lamp. Into darkness, indistinguishable from the fabric of the night.

I hear the shuffling of feet. I hear the panting of someone dying, the strangled groans of someone calling her name, the choking cries of ecstasy.

I know her well.

She is the one who sucks the sap from the young stem of love, licking milk from the swollen lips of men. She is the one who buries into soft flesh, searching for the very source of breath.

And afterwards, she disposes of them. As she did of me.

I drop the curtain and turn once more to my darkened room.

Cold

Jackie Davis

It was so cold. Jenna couldn't feel her hands. She had them tucked into the sleeves of her jersey and thrust, arms crossed, into her armpits, but she still couldn't feel them. *God, I hate winter.*

She sat on the wide ledge of the bay window. The roofs of the houses outside were metal arrowheads. Grey mostly. A cluster of dark green ones down in the new subdivision, the odd red one.

Jenna could hear her mother in the kitchen, baking bread. *Baking bread. Does she think this is still the seventies?* Jenna shivered. She tightened her hands into knots under her arms.

A trail of chimney smoke paused over one of the grey roofs. *They'll be warm.* The streets were almost empty. The off-to-work traffic had gone. Tech had started. Everyone was where they were supposed to be.

Jenna leaned her head against the window. Cold. She raised her head and looked at the patch where her forehead had left an imprint. Just a smudge really. She wanted to wipe away the coldness from her skin. It tickled. Jenna resisted the urge, concentrating instead on the sensation itself. Like tiny feet marching on the spot. Like the beginnings of a headache, on the outside, instead of inside her head. The feeling diminished. Now it was gone. She rubbed the place, just to make sure.

Outside, a tall tree shuddered.

Jenna breathed onto the window. Huhh. Her breath made a milky cloud on the glass. She watched its edges curl in on itself. Watched it get smaller and smaller. Watched it disappear. She breathed on the window again. She wrote her name in the cloud, pulling her hand out of the warmth of her armpit. J – E – N – N – A. It shrank. She watched the letters of her name fade, one by one.

'What are you doing, love?' Jenna's mother stood in the doorway, a vapour trail of flour across her forehead.

'Nothing, Mum. Just sitting. You know.' She turned back to the window, watched her reflection smile.

'I'm just in here, if you need me. In the kitchen.'

'I'm okay.' The words came out so naturally. Jenna sighed.

She breathed another cloud on the window. Drew a stick figure. A girl in a triangle skirt. Hair that stood up in straight lines. *Stick girl*. That disappeared too.

A fantail flittered outside. Hovered in front of Jenna, opened its tail. It dipped its head, then flew straight towards her. She could see the individual feathers on its tail, edged in white. It flew straight to her, thudded against the glass and fell onto the concrete below. It left a red smear on the window.

Huhh. Over the top of the blood stain. Huhh, again to go over the tail of it, sliding down the glass. Huhh, one more.

She raised her finger. Paused. C – O – L – D, she wrote. Watched as the edges slowly vanished. She shivered. She just couldn't warm up.

When You Go to San Francisco Be Sure to Wear Flowers in Your Hair

Margaret Crawford

Remember to smile. Say something that is positive. The afternoon fog spreads though the streets of San Francisco. She said she would come. I stand in the shadow and watch her walking between the cars. I can't see her face. Her hair is shorter than I remember. She seems taller. It hasn't been that long. Two years of calls, emails, a few letters to keep the cord that binds us alive. I remember to smile. She allows me to hug her.

When she was born the nurse raised her for me to see. With her head of dark hair, she was perfect. I can still feel, in those hours before dawn, her warmth as she nestled against my shoulder or suckled the breast.

'You look great.' I kiss her on the cheek. She smiles. I notice the ring through the nose.

'What have you for me?' I hear the little girl. I have not forgotten and hand her the parcel of surprises. The bar of chocolate, the silver ring, the coloured notebook. I am her mother again.

Night becomes a chessboard with moves and counter moves as we play the ritual. I will not hurt her. I counter each statement with a statement of my own. Her pawn for my pawn. We start with the small moves that at times leave us exposed. Other moves protect or remove the threat. We know the power we each hold. The ritual keeps us safe.

There's brittleness about her, a vulnerability. She holds her head high. She tells me how she has managed the lawyers. The joint counselling helped but he can't be trusted. He promised to pay her but nothing materialised. The debts are mounting.

On the day of their commitment he wore starry pants and a crown of flowers. The colour of her dress matched his shirt. We, who came to witness the ceremony, danced in circles in Golden Gate Park while another played the flute. We ate chocolate cake and drank cider. Friends read poetry. My golden girl and her lover promised to have a life filled with laughter and fun. He loved the magic. I thought she was so lucky to find a playmate. My little girl, playing in the sun.

She does not ask me to her house. In the morning I dress and walk the streets. I find myself in the street where she lives. There is her house. A rainbow flag covers the doorway.

Another meal. The chessboard lies in front of us. The wine in the glass catches the glow of the candle and breaks the light into a rainbow.

She says, 'I'm gay.'

Exposure. I move the bishop but do not checkmate her. I look down at the rainbow on the cloth.

The flags in the Castro district are rainbows flying in the wind and the fog begins to drift in. I kiss her on the cheek and hand her a ring of flowers to wear in her hair. I enter the departure lounge and look back to see her standing alone holding the flowers high as a salute.

Queen of the Snows

Tim Jones

I passed Burgess just above 7000 feet, halfway across the difficult traverse between Pearson Col and the Forgotten Icefall. It was clear he was struggling.

'What's wrong? Altitude sickness?'

'Briefcase too heavy.' He clasped it to him and struggled on.

The icefall is treacherous at the best of times, but today it was rotten with seracs and consultants. I saw a respected senior counsel almost carried off when a great horn of ice crashed down on the ledge he was crossing, and was forced to waste valuable time rescuing the Manufacturers' Association from a crevasse. I barely made it back onto firm snow by nightfall, and had to pitch my tent by moonlight.

I rose to a fair dawn and lost no time in striking camp. Weather like this was too good to waste. My breath froze before me as, with crampons and ice-axe, I toiled up the slope and onto the summit ridge, my eyes dazzled by the sun and the view.

I was on the summit almost before I knew it, and there she was: her flashing eyes, her floating hair, her laptop and satellite modem.

'Name?'

'Loveridge. I'm here about …'

'Inquiry, commission, inquisition? Choose wisely.'

'We were hoping for a select committee.'

She froze me with a look. 'A commission of inquiry will commence on this spot in two weeks, weather permitting. All participants should be represented by counsel. Dismissed.'

'But …'

'Two weeks. Be here at dawn.' I backed out of the Presence.

The thought of roping twenty lawyers together and shepherding them up the Forgotten Icefall was so appalling that I didn't notice Burgess until I was almost on top of him. He looked paler than ever.

'Got a moment? How did it go?' He sank gratefully onto the snow.

'Got what I came for. Back in two weeks.'

'What was she wearing?'

'A brown survival suit with a yellow outer jacket. A woolly hat and typing gloves. Is that enough to go on?'

'You realise that wasn't her?'

'Wasn't who?'

'You didn't meet the Queen. That was her secretary. She schedules meetings, but she doesn't make decisions. I,' said Burgess proudly, 'am meeting the Queen in thirty minutes.'

'You'd better hurry, then.'

It wasn't wise, and I paid for it later with a frantic descent in the half-dark; but there wasn't room to hide a postage stamp on that summit, and only one route that led there. To meet Burgess, the Queen had to pass me. Shivering in the rising wind, I watched him toil upward.

He was almost at the summit when she came. Borne aloft by her red and green plumage, uttering a single harsh cry, the Queen of the Snows wheeled once in the thin cold air before settling on her mountain throne.

Learning Greek

Adrienne Rewi

Mysterio is the Greek word for mystery. I learned this when Kosta disappeared. Six weeks ago, I woke up to the simplicity of another unspoiled Greek day and his side of the bed was cold, not even rumpled. He hadn't come home. He still hasn't come home.

There's a numbing silence in the village and even the rhythmic clip-clop of donkey hooves on cobbles seems eerily quieter. No one knows anything. No one has seen him.

Fovos is the Greek word for fear. I made sure I learned this when Kosta disappeared. I needed a way of telling the leathery-skinned fisherman how important it was that they think about Kosta and whether they might have seen him. But they all had a subdued certainty about them as they slicked their knives over fresh catches of fish and octopus.

I had walked away, winding up the cobbled hillside alleys, through a weaving of whitewashed houses and the heady scents of rosemary and orange blossom compressed into the hot, still air, despairing inside at ever finding my closest friend, my lover, my reason for being in Greece.

Okeanos is the Greek word for ocean. Kosta had taught me that as we'd sat together above the cliffs in sharp light that endowed even ordinary things with extraordinary beauty. The body of deep blue, Greece's Aegean – the harbourer of history, of legend, of secrets – spread out hundreds of feet below us, coming ashore in shades of crystalline blue on a tiny, cliff-backed beach of white sand. That's where we'd gone every afternoon, working our way down steep, rocky hillsides, through orange and olive groves, past the tiny tavernas cantilevered above the sea, to lie together, sweating and touching, before plunging into the all-knowing waters.

I didn't learn the word for geraniums, but they were everywhere, scattered scarlet. They filled old tin cans, a crumbling earthenware pot; they lined the paths to doorways and they glowed on rooftops and stairways, red cut-outs against endless blue.

Kosta taught me about *agapi* – love. Out retsina-fuelled laughter had rung through the hillside silence of cypress and ruins, bouncing back to us off old stone walls smothered in scrappy, sweet-smelling bushes of thyme and oregano. Our lazy days had been filled with no greater purpose than discovering each other; and as nights followed blood-red sunsets, our passions were the only urgency.

Lipi is the Greek word for sadness. I know this more deeply as each day of Kosta's disappearance remains unsolved. I won't leave until the sparkling white houses with their cool courtyards tumbled in scarlet bougainvillea and geraniums have given up their secrets. I know that white is not always pure; I know there are answers behind implacable faces; I know Kosta wouldn't leave without saying goodbye.

Yia sou is the Greek word for goodbye. But the Greeks use the same word for hello. There can be confusion, but not for me. I am more confused by *asaphia* – ambiguity.

Visiting Rights

Bridget Musters

'Double bed for sale.' The advertisement caught Rowan's eye. 'As new, six foot six inches long, only half used.' Which half, she wondered, his or hers? Or did the occupants curl up very small so only the top half was ever slept in? Was it a sign of inseparable passion? Or unrequited love? Rowan certainly didn't need such a long bed, but it was the only double in that day's paper, and sleeping in a single always made her feel ten years old. Anyway, there was never any harm in Being Prepared.

A man answered the phone and they arranged a time later in the day when she could go and see it.

When he opened the door Rowan could see why he'd needed that bed.

'It was made for me,' he said, 'and for the first time since I was thirteen I managed to sleep without my feet getting cold. The only problem is, it's too big for this house – I can't even get it up the stairs.' Ducking the door lintel, he led Rowan into the sitting room. The sofa and armchairs were squashed into the corners of the room. The bed was in the middle, and even seeing it denuded Rowan knew she had to have it. The rimu head and foot were smooth, and thicker than an arm. The corner curve ran down unjointed to the leg. She couldn't keep herself from stroking the polished wood.

Rowan felt the mattress with her fist.

'That was made specially, too,' he said. 'It's a futon, wool. Go on, try it. You can't buy a bed without lying on it first.'

She sat on the edge of the bed. Her side or his, she wondered, humming Dylan's *Lay Lady Lay*. Growing bolder, she lay down, ankles crossed. It didn't seem right somehow to curl up on her side – too like taking possession.

'Well, it's certainly very comfortable,' Rowan said.

'I'd really like it to go to a good home,' he said, as if he were talking about a slightly loved and suddenly inconvenient cat.

Some months later, Rowan ran into him at the cheese stall in the market.

'And how's the bed?' he asked.

'Oh, still only half-used,' she answered, 'but I don't know if it's the same half. Come and see it sometime.' He did, and brought his new partner with him, six feet tall, and very elegant. She came straight to the point.

'I don't suppose you'd consider selling the bed, would you, Rowan? I'd give you a good price for it. Much more than you gave Geoff for it.'

Rowan shook her head. 'Sorry. I've got quite fond of it now.' She patted the rimu foot rail. 'And I always live in hope.'

Geoff smiled as his partner turned away.

'I don't think she'll put up with cold feet for long,' he said, 'hers or mine.'

She didn't. Now Geoff's got warm feet again, and both sides of our bed are used.

Sunday at the Beach with George

Isa Moynihan

Kirksbridge is a polite and tidy place – at least it is where we live. It's different in the inner city, they say, especially at night. And there are suburbs where pit bulls roam, houses mysteriously burn down and babies are killed.

Beachville is also polite but slightly raffish, as seaside suburbs can be. On fine Sundays George and I often drive there after lunch. In summer it can become rather congested with traffic but there is still room for everyone on the beaches.

Last Sunday was a beautiful day, sun tempered by the sea breeze. We found our usual seat on the walkway above the rocks. Before us spread the postcard blue South Pacific with white waves breaking on a golden beach. Happy families basked and swam and threw striped balls to one another. We sighed with pleasure and took deep breaths of the fresh, salty air.

Along the walkway from our right a young man approached, pushing a child in a stroller. They were both quite black. Not a common sight in Kirksbridge. Something about the man said educated middle-class. (You can always tell, can't you?) We smiled at him as he passed. He smiled back. (Such dazzling teeth they have!) A woman followed them, a few paces behind. Her head was draped in a scarf, pulled forward to hide her face, her body hidden in a loose tunic with long sleeves, her legs invisible in baggy trousers caught in at the ankle. She didn't look at us.

'Muslim?' I suggested.

George nodded. 'Probably Somali,' he said.

They receded from us along the walkway. The sun was losing its heat, shadows growing longer. George and I also began our walk back.

Nearing the car park we noticed that a crowd had gathered, their backs to us. They seemed to be watching something – a busker, perhaps?

This crowd, though, seemed uneasy. A couple in front of us turned away shaking their heads and suddenly we could see what they'd been watching.

Our black man – the one we'd smiled at – was lying on the ground being kicked by a white youth with a shaved head and heavy boots. His friends stood round, cheering him on. The man's wife was screaming and so was their child in the pushchair. The man was trying to protect his head from the boots. No one went to help him.

Then, suddenly, it was all over. The youth stopped kicking the black man, and walked away, laughing with his friends. People made way for them.

The black man stood up. He looked at us one by one in the silence.

Then he said that where they came from there were places where you were safe one day but where you might be killed the next, depending on which group was in charge.

'So now we feel quite at home,' he said.

He put his arm round his wife and they too walked away.

Nor'wester

Tracey Edginton

They say looking after grannies can drive you nuts. Just like the Canterbury nor'westers.

They say that when the warm wind gathers up its skirts to dance its dull, aching tap in your head, people go crazy. They just up and kill themselves. The statistics prove it. The papers say that more suicides are committed in Christchurch when the nor'wester blows than at any other time of the year. You can ring the coroner's office to find out. You can't ask how they did it. Only when. Then it's just a matter of comparing it with the weather maps. That's what they say.

I fainted once in a nor'wester. There I was, drench gun in hand, a splash of red in a white, wintry four-legged world. The wind, caressing in its infancy, blowing its warm breath up my shorts. More intense now, lapping at my red bandanna, daring it to blow off my face. I let it blow. I didn't feel so good. The sheep could tell. They were leaning their weight against me, helping me stand. The wind was closing in. It was dancing in my head. The sheep couldn't hold me. Their whiteness engulfed me.

When I woke, the farmhouse had claimed me. Kate's mum sweet in her concern. 'You shouldn't be out there without a hat. Not when the wind's blowing like that.'

It's the same over here if you look after grannies. It can drive you nuts. Just like the wind.

Only Kiwis can handle it. That's why rich English grannies pick us, because of our colonial spirit. We never studied New Zealand history at school, but it means that we don't mind hard work.

I heard of one girl who was attacked by her granny with a knife. And all over a sandwich. The ones like we have at home made her granny sick. They didn't actually make her vomit. The sheer size put her off eating.

That granny was an alcoholic. They sent her away. Dad's an alcoholic. Maybe they should send him away?

My Nana's face, draped with skin tags like a pair of badly hung curtains, pops into my head. 'Beggars can't be choosers,' she says.

Dad's put her in her place. He's telling her all right. 'Don't feed that proverb crap to me. You've no sooner said, "He who hesitates is lost" than you're preaching, "Look before you leap".'

He was clever, Dad. Had an answer for everything.

'Forty thousand dollars worth of private education and you want to look after some old granny?'

He wanted me to take the job at the newspaper.

Twenty-two with the ink of a two-year working visa fresh in my passport. I was safe from my future. A sole blue stamp in a blank book, a clean piece of paper to decorate the way I wanted.

But I reckon it could drive you nuts. The wind I mean. I've only ever fainted once.

It's too cold in London for nor'westers.

Departure

Stephen Stratford

It had been a long day. There was the Taiwanese business delegation, the Japanese tour party and then an entire Samoan village, laughing and crying after a family wedding in Auckland. Tania had ten minutes to go before the end of her shift on the information desk, and now this. Some sweating, red-faced middle-aged guy babbling about how he had to get this bottle of pills to a passenger who'd already boarded her flight. Yeah, right. We do this all the time. Not a problem.

First she was his wife, then no, his partner, like Tania cared, but whatever she was she really really needed these pills. Though when she thought about it, Tania also hated a long haul without sleeping pills, so she could understand. You could see they were just pills, not a bomb or heroin or anything. So hoping she wasn't making a big mistake, she relented. 'I'll try. That's all I can promise,' she said, and you could see the guy practically wet himself with gratitude.

This was the last time. He was out of there. Going to the airport Robyn had been her craziest yet. They were late to leave because she'd dithered over what clothes to take, then halfway over the Mangere bridge she'd started rootling through her bag then wailing that she'd left her sleeping pills behind, so she wouldn't sleep on the flight, so when she got to LA she'd be exhausted and stressed, so she wouldn't be able to function. Christ she hated her life, she shouted, hitting her thighs again and again, then the armrest and the roof. She'd fucked it all up, fucked up everything in her life, everything, and she couldn't even catch a plane without it being a disaster.

Now she was howling. He'd thought people did that only in books.

'It's all right, love,' he said. 'Easily fixed. I'll drop you off, go home, get the pills and bring them to the airport. It'll only take half an hour. See you by the check-in counter.' Over the harbour bridge and back at 130kph the whole way, diving in and out of lanes, cutting in on the big rigs, tailgating anyone in his way, driving like the aggressive drunken teenage hoon he'd never been. He'd felt the fear and done it anyway, and now he was wringing.

Michael drove slowly home, lay down on the bed and began to shake.

'Have you heard about Robyn? Michael's left her. She's very upset. Well, obviously.'

'God. They've been together, what, five years?'

'Six. Nearly as long as with Tim.'

'She does have bad luck. And in between there was that American.'

'Yes. And the lawyer – Duncan?'

'Derek. Mind you, I always thought Michael wasn't quite …'

'The weird thing was that he must have been in a hurry – just took his golf clubs and CDs. She came home to a letter on the kitchen table. Something about the airport.'

'A letter. Typical. Men are such cowards.'

Falling

Diane Brown

On the night before Denise is due to fly home they sit in a popular café and watch the customers arriving. Stars after dark. 'It's like an Emily Perkins story,' Denise says, 'only grottier.' Jim nods. Denise is pleased she doesn't have to explain who Emily Perkins is. Jim is literate and sexy; for Denise, an attractive combination.

In the corner of the café a large person of indiscriminate sex lurches out of her seat and stumbles past. Her eyes are glazed, her movements slow, exaggerated by her skirt, long and stiffened satin, a dusky pink. Salmon, Denise supposes. And on drugs.

A thin girl wanders in and hugs the lank boy sporting a purple velvet cloak. She hops from one leg to the other, trying to keep warm or dissipate an excess of energy. Maybe she hasn't got a wardrobe, thinks Denise, or maybe it's her lack of fat that causes her to layer on clothes, two skirts and three tops of different colours and lengths, all so faded, they merge into one another. On her head a pink crocheted pixie hat. Denise thinks of Jed, her son, who lately has taken a fancy to his baby hat. The only one she ever made. White, with a multicoloured border and long flaps to tie around his neck. Flaps were necessary. He was the sort of child who was always trying to pull off his clothes and run away. Now he is sixteen and the only boy at college who would dare to wear such a hat to school. She has seen the way the other pupils look admiringly at him. Especially the girls.

'Jed wears a hat like that,' Denise points out. 'Really,' Jim says and frowns. Perhaps he is worried she will start talking about Jed's friend Ben. Such a stupid death. Falling off a cliff, two months ago. Denise can't get the picture out of her mind. She's dreamt of falling, for years now. Down cliffs and mines, even lifts. Sometimes her, sometimes Jed.

She wonders if it is because Jed is an only child. She wonders why it was Ben and not Jed who fell.

'It's about time Jed grew up,' Jim says. 'Time you let him go and moved in with me, where you could work in peace.' Denise is a potter. She makes blue angels. 'But it's the other end of the country,' Denise says. 'And he's only sixteen.'

The girl in the pixie hat raises her voice. 'Did you hear, I nearly died?'

'*No*,' says the boy in the purple cloak.

'Yeah, gas poisoning. In the caravan. I was out to it. They took an hour to wake me up. Scary as.'

'Ready?' Jim says. He is already standing, pulling on his hat. Denise tries to think of all the things she wants to say, before it is too late.

In the car, she says, 'I was listening to a girl who nearly died. Gas poisoning.'

'Really?' Jim says. 'What girl? The only girl I noticed was you. I was thinking about your angels. How they seem to be fashionable at the moment but at some time you need to move on. Bowls, perhaps. Have you any ideas?'

'No,' says Denise. She is thinking about the plane tomorrow, dropping out of the sky. About sleeping alone again, for who knows how long. About Jed, smiling in his multicoloured hat, before her recurring dreams started. At the time he began walking, she now realises.

'True Facts About Girls Who Smoke and Drink Liquor'

Jane Bissell

My mother taught me to drink. At first it was wine with dinner, then we moved on to spirits.

'You need to know how to drink responsibly,' she said, 'and with a sense of style.'

My mother, BJ, grew up in a small coastal Florida town during the 1940s. One day, her white-haired, sea captain grandpa handed her mother a booklet he thought might help BJ to 'plot a course' through the hazards of adolescence. It was called *True Facts About Girls Who Smoke and Drink Liquor*. After a thorough perusal, the book was given to BJ. The lessons contained therein about alcohol and other subjects have stayed with her.

My mother considered some drinks to be universally acceptable and 'safe' when socialising.

'Gin and tonic is always a good bet,' she said, 'or brandy, lime and soda. And of course you can always ask for a slug of good scotch, with ice and a splash.'

But her real favourites were mint juleps and martinis. These were notorious for their potency. Her daddy taught her how to mix them, but only after she was married. My mother insisted on the best bourbon for her mint juleps, and the driest vermouth and gin for her martinis. She loved vermouth so much, she often said she could wear it behind her ears, like perfume.

She mixed her martinis in a cut glass pitcher with ice, stirred with a glass rod, and served with green olives on toothpicks. Or, on hot summer afternoons, she would prepare a batch of mint juleps. She made these in solid silver goblets frosted with ice from the freezer. The cracked ice, sugar syrup, bourbon and fresh mint melted down into a deliciously icy mix, which we would sip under the shade of a spreading pohutukawa in the back yard.

'Now this is some stylish drinking,' she would say.

In her mid-fifties, my mother developed Parkinson's disease. It began as a trembling in her left hand, then spread to both arms and hands. She would say back then the trembling was 'mighty fine' for mixing up martinis. Now, in her late sixties, she is frail and forgetful and relies more and more on what she calls her 'strong Southern heritage' to pull her through the ups and downs of the disease.

My mother and I still enjoy a drink together. Heady days of martinis and mint juleps have mellowed into glasses of wine or sherry by a warm, winter fire. She misses those powerful drinks of hers, showing off the art her daddy taught her, getting just the right balance of ice and liquor. The skill is now beyond her.

But, as always, my mother shows a genteel Southern grace, accepting her deteriorating condition with dignity and humour. She raises her glass with both hands, gazing thoughtfully at the golden liquid. 'I don't feel the same way about sherry,' she said. 'Behind my ears, I mean.'

Step Forward, Step Back

Sarah Quigley

She was big. Sitting in a seat all day behind a gear stick had built her up, and out. She thought of herself as Amazonian, he just called her big. As big as a bus, he'd said when he first heard what she did for a job. She loved him even though his jokes were over-obvious.

He was small. His neck scragged from his body like a turtle; he walked with small bowed steps. They both did things around the house, but their domestic life was shaped by their physiognomies. He superglued cracked dishes, she relocated walls. Their relationship was equable, equal.

When he asked her what she wanted for her thirtieth, she couldn't say. She held her breath.

'Spit it out,' he said.

She was used to bellowing the names of bus stops so he flinched a bit.

'What the hell is a stole?' he asked.

'How the hell can I afford mink?' he asked.

'Where the hell would you wear it?' he asked.

She knew he loved her, though.

On her birthday morning he brought her coffee and Marmite toast. He always put the butter on too thick, reminding her of his sense of humour. She realised relationships were a series of compromises.

'Want your pressie now?' he said.

'Okay,' she said.

'I *stole* it for you,' he said significantly. He winked.

She went outside to wait in the sun. She felt quite festive and stuck a white flower behind her ear like a bride. She looked at the unfenced garden, thought vaguely of white trellises.

'Coming ready or not,' he sang.

She stood on the veranda with her huge arms over her eyes. The undersides of her arms were white and smooth, and as soft as fur.

She heard puffing, a thump.

'You can look,' he told her.

A coil of fencing wire sat on the path in front of her. He'd tied a purple ribbon round it.

Gears shifted in her head, graunched.

'What's the matter?' he said.

She thought hard of the hard vinyl seat at her back, the comfort of the moving floor under her work shoes.

'Hey, it's not really stolen,' he said.

'Why are you crying?' he said.

'For God's sake!' he said.

Silver wire ran, slipped, into the concrete path. She looked up. The clouds streaked the sky, running fast like small white animals.

'You know I bloody love you,' he said.

Eve and Adam

Bernard Steeds

Blood, which had congealed brown on the carpet, slowly dissolved to form a red pool and rose up in the air, coming first in a few faint drips, then in a faster, spiralling flow. With a mortal grunt he lifted himself to his knees. A deep slash crossed his neck, like a big red smile. The blood flowed into the wound, and skin healed from right to left as if it was a plastic zipper being drawn. She pulled the blade back and plunged it into her pocket. Then she withdrew her arm from around his head. He rose from his knees into the chair, his movements those of a puppet, involuntary and formless, against gravity. Carefully, without breathing, she walked backwards across the room, her footsteps making no sound. She stepped around a coffee table and a leather couch without difficulty or hesitation, and went through the doorway without looking where she was going. Her eyes were fixed on the back of his head. She remained hidden in the shadows while he sat in his chair, writing, 'Redundant now is man. Turned has history of tide the'. He leaned away from the desk. Whisky rose from his stomach, burning his throat. He swirled it over and under his tongue and spat it into a glass, which he placed carefully on the desk beside his papers. He scratched his chin. He sighed. It was nothing. He looked across the room, then turned back to his work. He thought he heard a sound. She could see him through the open doorway.

This man, a historian, wrote of Hitler and Stalin and Pol Pot, and sometimes also of Henry VIII and his daughter Elizabeth. He believed, and told his students, that 'history is a pulse, pumped by a primate heart'. He meant by this that man was flawed and complex but his impulses – ultimately – were simple, which he knew because, as he stood in the lecture hall, between blackboard and blank eyes, he could not help himself from scanning for pretty girls. When his pen marked the page with ancient Roman symbols, and commas, full stops and colons, his quest was not truth but immortality. And, though he hated his job and would leave in an instant if he could, he would just as happily flare his nostrils, beat his foot on the ground, charge headlong at, and clash heads with, any other beastly professor who came before him in the mortal battle for tenure.

The woman was an agent of the future. She knew in her heart that the light of gravity was flickering, and oceans were on the move. Where once a wave crashed atop another, now the lower wave rose and arched back, pulling away the ocean like a scab, revealing a landscape of shadow and rib, which was her Eden.

Spain-ish Hearts

Katy Dugdale

If you tilt your head slightly to the left and squint, you can see the sea. Right over there, between those two swaying palms. Its smell is everywhere.

We have rented an apartment for two weeks. It has an ocean view and is going to save our marriage.

Brian sits on the veranda a lot with his head tilted to the left and I lie on the bed, doing the same.

I keep falling asleep and dribbling on the crocheted coverlet. My face gets all lumpy and marked from its pattern. I am having dreams that are meant for other places, other beds, which wake me with a start.

So does Brian's voice.

The TV channels here are not in English. At night we watch Spanish love and war with the sound off. Then listen to it live, outside with vespers and Catalan whores.

If you are very quiet in the mornings and listen outside our door, with your head tilted slightly to the right, you can hear two hearts breaking. With every breath exhaled, we expel a little more of each other.

We have one week left in paradise and are in extreme pain. Neither of us wants to be here; each is scared to leave alone.

I make friends with the girls in the brothel downstairs and Brian is appalled.

Two of them drink with us at sunset on our veranda and Brian is intrigued. They arrive every night. Their company is exquisite. They are our beautiful girls and we anticipate their coming like Christmas.

I go out late to the bars with them and Brian is confused.

I should tell him I have no need for him to understand me. We are ephemeral. I hold for him neither landmark nor anchors.

We watch a porn channel and get only uncomfortable, even with the sound on. This is bad. The woman looks like me. Worse, the man looks like my lover.

Brian takes a long shower. It is my turn to feel left out.

If you stand under our place at midnight, with your chin tilted slightly upward, you will see wine dripping from our veranda ledge, and the moon reflected on broken glass, and the sound of two whores weeping.

The Sack Man

Michael Bland

He felt uncomfortable in the marble-floored foyer with its reflective tile walls that only made his uniform glow brighter.

The receptionist showed no recognition when he offered his name. Wearing bright red lipstick that matched the colour of his suit, she pointed towards a leather couch in front of a tall oak door set in a chunky aluminium frame. Above the brass door handle a gold plate read: Morgan Babcock, Director of Marketing.

'Mr Babcock will be with you in a moment,' said the hair-in-a-bun receptionist, her eyes lingering on his suit just a little too long. Buried in the big brown couch, he must have looked like a half-eaten Jaffa, he thought. He sat quietly, staring down at his black ankle length boots – or what little he could see of them over the concave curve of his belly.

As he fidgeted nervously with the frilly tassels at the base of his sleeves, an invisible air-conditioning system hummed gently, filling the air with a chill that was nothing like the friendly cold he knew back home. He'd been dreading this meeting for weeks. He disliked the city and its contents, except, of course, the children. It was a shame some would grow up to be bastards like Babcock.

At 2.15pm – thirty minutes after the meeting was scheduled to start – a polished black phone on the reception desk burped twice. 'Mr Babcock will see you now.'

He extracted himself from the couch with some difficulty, a bead of sweat forming among the dense white curls on his head and trickling downwards over a red, vein-tracked cheek.

The meeting took ten minutes and as expected contained the usual marketing jargon that Babcock had patronised him with ever since the business was privatised. 'My research department tells me you're just not cutting it with the key demographics any more,' Babcock droned. 'My marketing analysts say your transport and distribution system is prehistoric, and our sponsors aren't at all happy with your uncooperative attitude. And my public relations people tell me you don't have the image that sells today. Frankly, you're way too fat and you've refused to wear the new suit provided by our fashion consultants.'

He knew it was over so the rest was a blur except those three final R words – restructuring, redundancy, replacement.

Head sagging, the old man shuffled through the ground-level car park towards a red Toyota Landcruiser emblazoned with the slogan 'Coruba: The Spirit of Christmas'. Two cars away was a dark Porsche coupe with the number plate 'Babs1'. He delved into the trouser pocket of his red suit and pulled out his keys.

They made a piercing squeal as they peeled a thin strand of paint from the bonnet to the boot. But he didn't care. He'd never spent Christmas at home before.

The Flat Rock Club

Jon Thomas

He wouldn't go. Couldn't, he told her. It was an apology, sort of. 'I'm fitting doors today.' Like there'd be no tomorrow if he didn't. All the time wiping his hands on a rag that had once, years ago, been her pyjama top. She recognised the pattern.

He left her nothing to say and she wandered back into the house. Unless he was off somewhere looking for parts, he worked on the car every weekend – a 1934 Chevy he'd picked up a year back for next to nothing from some farmer he met in the pub. What started out a hobby had become a passion. No, an obsession. Bloody car was all he ever thought about.

Earlier, he'd said he *would* go, and that made it worse. She wanted to go fishing at Flat Rock. 'You remember? We used to go down there all the time,' she said.

'Of course I remember,' he said. He grinned.

They had made love there once. On the rock. In the sunshine.

She thought about going alone, but then her eyes kept filling up. She couldn't settle to anything. He was hammering in the garage. Then Della arrived.

'Just dropped in for a chat,' she said. 'You look as if you need cheering up. At least you know where he is,' she said.

'Where's Greg then?'

'Some pub somewhere. Who the hell cares?' Della made it sound like a joke, but she didn't laugh.

In the end the two woman went to Flat Rock together. 'Who needs them anyway,' Della said.

And after clambering down the cliff to get onto the rock, and her thinking stupidly that he might be there, might have somehow overtaken them, they found there *was* someone there: a woman, a stranger, hunched up over her line.

'Mind if we fish alongside you? We'll try not to get tangled.'

The woman shrugged. She didn't even look up. They moved along the rock, as far from her as they could and both caught a kahawai on their first cast out. 'They're bloody hungry today,' she shouted, and thought, this has to be more fun than fixing up a stupid motorcar.

Della called out to the stranger, 'You're in the wrong place, honey.'

The woman ignored her. She appeared not to have noticed the noise they were making or the fish flapping on the rock but continued to stare into the ocean as she had all along, and then, as if mysteriously signalled, began winding her line in, slowly, hand over hand, expertly, until she had it all and they saw she had just a sinker attached. No hooks, no tackle.

'You lost your gear. Must have been a big one, eh?'

The woman smiled awkwardly, and they saw the bruises on her face. 'You have to look as if you're doing something, don't you, though?' she said.

Their House Up North

Jane Blaikie

A fringe of rug, trailing a day bed, trembles. The guinea pig is freed from the arms of a child asleep beneath the bed and it nibbles a tassel. Its nub of tongue pushes aside the thread; it shakes its head, steps out, sniffs and looks around in a dim short-sighted way.

In the furthest corner a larger boy lifts his slug gun, takes aim. But the little ruminant acts on instinct, and motors across the faded carpet like a slipper on paddles and squeezes beneath a wooden chest.

The gun lowers. Rising from an armless chair, the larger boy slowly walks the length of the long sun room toward a glass door opening onto lawns. He says, 'Wouldn't waste the ammo.'

He wears army fatigues, and when his stepmother asks him not to and bundles them into charity bins, he uses his allowance to buy more.

After he has gone, leaving the door open, bird song and breezes waft in. Eventually, the guinea pig's twitching nose emerges and it waddles a criss-cross path down the patterned carpet and out into the garden.

A blowfly comes in and buzzes the sash windows.

Under the bed, the small child's eyes open. He lies listening to the birds and the trees in the wind until he sees his empty hands. Rolls them into closed fists; bangs the carpet's bound edge. He crawls out, sees the far door is open, and after looking under the chest, he too goes into the garden.

For a while the room is empty; then a woman enters from the main part of the house. She sits in the armless chair and begins to weep, her sniffs rising to short howls with her head hunched. After the fourth howl, she stops to blow her nose.

When she looks up the older boy is framed by the garden door, still holding his gun.

He idles closer, 'Did ya hear then, Cilla? Is he coming?'

Cilla looks from one door to the other as if someone might appear. 'He can't come, Jeremy. There's a problem with the float, it's lingerie and the tariffs … He has to change …'

'And?'

'He's hoping to be clear. Not for this weekend, Jeremy. For the weekend after.'

The boy shouts, 'What did ya say, Cilla? Silly Cilla. Did ya moan?'

Cilla stands, tall and bony with it. She walks up very close to the boy, her chin level to his ear, which has a fine coating of blonde hairs. 'Next week,' she says. 'We have to wait until next week.'

She looks past him and sees her own child at the garden door. She whispers to Jeremy, 'I want you to put the gun away. Lock it away now.'

The child at the door calls: 'Lost Carrot, Mum. Carrot run away.'

The older boy sneers, but backs away toward the inner part of the house.

Cilla kneels by her son, who says, 'Find Carrot, Mum.'

Expunging God

Bronwyn Tate

Kit is hoping for a chance, he says as he takes the narrow road towards the summit of Mt Eden, to talk to the boys. A chance Monica knows will not come. The city opens up beneath them as they climb, a collage of line and colour, of streets and trees and angled roofs. Faded confetti.

The car park undulates with heat, vaporising distant bodies as they ascend towards the viewing platform. Monica finds a spot of shade beneath the pines, away from the children, from Kit, and from the crowds. Cicadas sing descant to the exclamations of Japanese tourists, and the snapping of cameras. The city high-rise is clear-edged, framed by the harbour with its seabird flock of yachts, Rangitoto, and beyond, the ocean. The sky is blue without blemish, revolving 360 degrees.

Monica slips off her sandals and digs her bare toes into the shining grass, feeling the warmth of the earth beneath.

The boys descend the crater, envious of others, more prepared, who skim down on old frayed sheets of cardboard. At its foot 'GOD' is sculpted in the grass with rocks. A boy reclines thoughtfully in the O. The air is alive with foreign inflection as he sets about expunging God. His friend, aware of a captive audience at the crater's lip, begins to formulate a message of his own.

Sean and Jack spy abandoned scraps of cardboard, and scuttle down to retrieve them, while Kit queues beside the ice-cream van. GOD is reduced to COD as the boys reach their goal, snatching up the frayed sheets and beginning their climb back towards the summit. Jack glances up and Monica waves, ignoring his look of entreaty, almost lost by distance. Manipulating mother by remote. COD becomes OD, as Sean, daunted by the steepness of the crater wall, waits for Jack. From habit Monica's eyes follow Kit, and she feels his impatience, and wonders whether the events of the night have freed him.

OD becomes OI as the boys reach the top and prepare to slide. Jack waves, enjoying the altered perspective, his mother reduced to a colourful speck on a hillside, his father steaming beside an ice-cream van. They hesitate, while Sean urges Jack to go first. The crater wall seems almost vertical from where they sit. Jack resists. It is his birthright to follow Sean's intrepid lead, his safety guaranteed.

OI is now O, now U, now J. The accomplice, assured of his originality, completes with a flourish, the K of FUCK.

The ice-creams liquefy as Kit comes back, and the boys leave their toboggans at the top without regret. How can Monica tell them that danger does not lurk in precipitous volcanic craters, but in their father's heart instead, in a marriage that suddenly finds itself devoid of love?

She notices as they prepare to leave that, in the unpigmented grass of the crater wall, God lives on. Their marriage, it seems, will not.

The Lighthouse

Grant Dale

We called it the lighthouse, Gary and I. It isn't really a lighthouse, but it is tall and lighthouse-like, and it is on a small beach by the end of the mole, so what else were us kids going to call it? Four eroded corner beams rise from glistening dark sand, high enough to support three layers of diagonal cross beams. The wood is grey and old, an occasional iron bolt adding a stain of rust, the top layer decorated in the streaky remains of white paint. Topping it off there is a platform, a platform of treasures – a rusted tumble of winch cogs, an old pulley on the end of a hooked metal rod, and a small shelter that from a distance looks like a weathered fruit box standing on its end.

The yellow sign is still there: DANGER – KEEP OFF. I ignore it now, as we both did then. A home-made ladder starts half way up the structure as if it were a fire escape. I scramble up to the first rung, and, testing each one as I go, climb to the top.

I look inland. I see tyre-lined wharves, idle tugs, a proud container ship. I see beleaguered church spires, upstart office buildings, a hazy glimpse of suburbia flowing into gentle farmland and the brown, folded velvet of the hills. This is my world, always has been. I like it here. Gary didn't feel the same. He had always looked out over the sea, past the tripod buoy far enough distant to make us wonder whether anyone could possibly swim to it, past the fishing boat pitching and rolling in a deceptively gentle swell, even past the horizon with its illusionary curve and faint fire glow.

It was what couldn't be seen from the lighthouse that interested Gary. He lived in a different world from me, one I could only wonder about through his postcards and the occasional email. His world was a place where exciting things seemed to happen every day, where money was plentiful at times and nonexistent at others, where the most amazing sights would loom out of mists and sunrises, never to leave the viewer the same again.

But now he is gone. Split-second timing and feverish traffic have conspired against him – he will never tell his story about a near miss. It's not easy to know what to do when a good friend dies. So now I sit on top of the lighthouse and gaze out at the world. The sea and what is over it will always be his, the land and what is on it will always be mine, and the lighthouse and all that it stands for will always be ours.

The Lives of Bryan

John McCrystal

TAYLOR, Bryan. Awesome digger-driver, fishing buddy and 'the man'. From Boss to Backfill. Will be missed by Darryl and Tamati of The Drain Brain.

TAYLOR, Bryan. Inspirational pastor of West Auckland Order of Divine Antinomians. Whosoever believeth in me.

TAYLOR, Bryan June 30. Father of Sally, Gayleen, Michelle, Rochelle, Karryn and Sindy. Stepdad of Shelly and Tahnya. Justice is mine, saith the Lord.

TAYLOR, Bryan. Stalwart of Henderson Hawks Rugby League Football Club. A big gap in the defensive line.

TAYLOR, Bryan. My Mr Fixit and special soulmate. Rest in peace, Twinkles. All my love, your Cuddlebuns.

TAYLOR, Bryan. Tireless member of Western Districts Drainage Board. The Board wish to extend their sympathy to Gaye and the kids.

TAYLOR, Bryan. Ex of Maureen, stepdad of Trevor, Shells and Tahns. Judge not, and be not judged.

TAYLOR, Bryan. A founding member of V8 Holdens for the Lord has taken the off-ramp to Zion.

TAYLOR, Bryan. Dad to Dwayne, Wayne, Mark, Tony, Carlos, Sid and the late Mike. Stepdad to Trevor. A diamond in the rough.

TAYLOR, Bryan Peter Maccabees (suddenly, at Swanson) June 30, aged 58 years. Husband of Gaye, ex-husband of Maureen, Helen and the late Dora. Dad and stepdad of many children. Bryan's service will be held at the West Auckland Divine Antinomians Hall (Railside Auto Salvage) on Sunday at 2pm, followed by a private cremation. Despise not the work of thy hands, O Lord. In lieu of flowers, donations to NZ Women's Refuge would be appreciated.

Going to Town

Victoria Cleal

Grandad's at the kitchen table, looking out the window. He's forgotten his rollie. Its tower of ash is about to crumble over his fingers. 'The Hemara kid's coming back from the butcher's. Chops, I bet. Cheap.'

He's got both bars of the heater on and his jumper's pushed up; on his left arm Melissa can see the wrinkly smear someone said was once a kiwi. He turns around when the cat butts him and boots it with his slipper. Ash scatters on the tablecloth.

'Where's the old trout? Where's your Nana?' he asks Melissa.

Melissa is glad when Nana comes in. She is wearing her court shoes and stockings, her tweed skirt and smart tan coat. The same every time, her going-to-town clothes. And pink lipstick. Nana looks at the ash on the tablecloth, looks at the scarf in her hands.

'What do you want to go out for in this bloody wind? Eh? Wasting money. Bloody stupid.' Grandad's hair stands up angrily but his face pulls down, melted. His blue eyes are surprised to be in such a face.

'Are you ready, Melissa?' Nana wraps the scarf around her perm, like gauze over a cake. 'We'll be back by five,' she tells Grandad. 'I'll bring a few slices of ham.'

He chokes up a cough. 'Yeah.'

Melissa buttons her coat up and they're off.

Down the side of the state house, Melissa dragging her hands on the grey asbestos board. The wind wants to push her back inside.

'We'll go to Kirk's,' Nana says.

Down the thirty steps. You can see all of Tawa from here, and the hill on the other side. There are more trees on the other side. Past the Morris Minor that doesn't work now, around a big red dog licking a tin on the footpath. Past the house with a black hole, chewed out by fire.

At the end of the street, Nana adds, 'And we'll have afternoon tea somewhere. Do you prefer scones or pikelets?'

They don't sit in the shelter at Kenepuru station because it smells like wee and there's a teenage boy there smoking.

'I need new gloves,' Nana says. 'And I'll buy you a book, if you don't tell Grandad.'

The train comes on time. Melissa kneels on the seat and breathes on the window, but Nana makes her sit down like a proper young lady. You have to be proper in town. You have to go to shiny shops and unfold huge towels, sniff soaps wrapped in ribbons, hold up fruit bowls and watch the light slide inside them like water. Boring. Nana never ends up buying these things, just a treat for Melissa.

The train goes around the corner and Melissa can see the grey house. 'Wave at Grandad!' says Melissa.

Nana looks up, but too quickly to really see anything. She is smiling, looking around for the ticket collector. 'We're away laughing,' she says.

To Hide the Hook

Garry P. Sommerville

All afternoon the tin boat has sat, rocked only by the occasional passing wake. The occupants are equally static. Fishing is slack, but Matt's keen to test some new equipment.

'See this,' he says, proffering the bent piece of spring, 'feel that strength.' It takes a mighty squeeze with old hands to force the steel jaws together enough to fit in fishy mouth. 'Squeeze together, stick it in their gobs, release and their mouths are forced open and you retrieve your hook.'

An untried weapon, normally with each rounded end resting inches apart. But the snapper are scarce, the kahawai coy. And Matt has a time limit. A wife of many years waiting ashore, angry that he is having fun while she wrestles with the housework.

'Hey! I'm on.' And for Matt the hours of boredom are bearing fruit. Bitter fruit. For his catch reveals itself as an angry greenish streak, churning into treacherous knots.

'Bloody moray, cut it off, that hook'll never catch anything now.' Terry offers the traditional wisdom.

'No, I'm gonna have that hook back.' Grunting with effort Matt forces the steel together and into the writhing shape on the line. With a snap the jaws are released springing open, for a clear view of the hell inside the awful creature.

Terry won't touch it, but holds the opener while Matt does the extraction. Which gives him a close up of the ghastly thing and its poisonously coloured mouth. He eyeballs the eel as Matt reaches for the hook. The eel fixes its wild eyes on Terry, and with a look of dreadful resignation slowly closes its mouth, forcing the steel jaws closed again until the power in the weapon punches one end through a primeval brain and the other bursts through the monster's lower jaw. Both men start in surprise, trying ineffectually to avoid the bloody soup squirting out of the primitive head.

'Jesus. Suicide. The bastard went sideways.' But Terry is silent, unable to forget the helpless despair in the glare fixed on him and the steady deliberate crunch on the deathly steel.

'Yuck, let's get outta here and clean this shit off.' Matt's keen to go now. He's tried his toy, and he's worried about his reception. 'A day wasted and no fish. She's not gonna be pleased.'

The journey back is silent. Terry musing over the eel's determination, and Matt apprehensive about his welcome. With the boat back on the trailer they trundle up to Matt's, where Sally is straight into battle.

'Had a good time, you useless bastard? On your arse drinking beer, while I'm slaving away at this ratpit.' Her voice rises as she reaches full stride and bile sprays the unfortunate husband wriggling like something on a hook.

Terry tries to ignore it, he's heard it all before, but he feels ashamed for his cowering mate. He shoots a quick glance, catching Matt's eye. And recognises in that eye a familiar frantic search for deathly steel to bite into.

Dahlias

Doug Coutts

'No, no, no, no, no, no – no!' Brian knocked the whole bunch off the table. A few stray red petals wafted down, otherwise the dahlias landed intact. Whump.

'I don't know how many times I have to say this,' he went on. 'Roses are fine, carnations are great. But no fucking dahlias. Got it?'

The PA turned the same shade as the flowers, scooped them up and left. To the closing door he shouted, 'They have no smell. What self-respecting flower has no smell?'

I was standing waiting for the bus. It was another cold morning and the wind was blowing straight up from the beach. Cold air and sand blasted my knees.

The satchel straps were starting to cut into my shoulder. I had too much in it already – library book, homework, pencil case, lunch and cordial – without the extra weight of the peanut butter jar.

'What's in the jar?' Ashley's big brother asked. Ron caught the same bus but he got off at the college stop.

'Nothing.'

'Then why's it got a paper lid?'

'It's a caterpillar.' I'd seen this caterpillar in one of the dahlia heads and Dad had thought it'd be good for the nature table. He'd put the whole head – along with some extra leaves for food – in the jar, covered the top with greaseproof and punched holes in it for air. Now I had to lug it all the way to school.

Ron had a look. 'It's big,' he said. 'What sort is it?'

I shrugged. A whole army of caterpillars could munch their way through the dahlias for all I cared.

A couple takes advantage of the weak winter sun to get into the garden. As they work along the row, lifting the bulbs and putting them in the wooden tomato boxes, a boy kicks himself back and forth on a tubular steel swing. He hates this – the droning of distant lawnmowers and nearer adult conversation, the smell of freshly turned soil and that whole Sunday afternoon feeling as another weekend disappears with nothing done or to do.

Postcard

Rachel Buchanan

(for Frances)

Dora Rigby likes to keep fit and active. Yesterday she mowed the
nature strip. It's the size of a Turkish rug but the only colour on it is
green. The sound of the blades reminded Dora of the sound of a
hundred needles hammering squares of cotton at the old mill in
Coburg. The mill girls made smalls for the boys in North Africa. Dora
stitched gussets and slipped friendly notes into the Y-fronts. She fell
in love daily, hourly, with the pictures in her mind. Camel racing,
pyramids, long brown legs. A cup of tea in a glass with a ring of gold
around the rim. Morse code, telegraph poles. Messages bucking and
tearing through the air, flapping and folding, like sheets on a line.

Dora's shoulders were her semaphore; they signalled her
intentions. When the right shoulder rose a little beneath the fluted
georgette, that meant Dora was becoming impatient with the young
man's talk. But if the right shoulder rose a little, then a little more, up,
up towards the marcasite fern attached to the right ear, then it meant
the young man should take her by the arm and lead her out of the
Preston Scout Hall and into the bluestone night. When she pushed
both shoulders back it meant she was mad. If her shoulders dropped
forward, then that meant she was thinking of her little sister Alice,
who got killed that day in Mildura when the buggy horse shied.

Dora still talks with her shoulders but only to the neighbours
now. She is nearly blind, so the people in the street are outlines to her
– a row of pastry-cutters who shout 'Hello' and reverse cars out of
driveways. Because Dora can no longer see much, she wonders if she
herself is seen.

She tucks a handkerchief under the strap of her sundress. A white flag of surrender. Help! She smells her lipstick to find the right colour. Rose is sweeter than plum. The maroon is furry like the inside of a slipper.

A postcard arrives. On the front Dora sees a smudge of yellow and orange — a sunset, a beach ball, the outback even. On the back, a whole lot of chicken scratchings. She takes her spy glass out of her pocket and pushes it in towards the writing. The word 'Love' spreads out like a raindrop on a window and it makes Dora's face damp.

Sparklers

Tamzin Blair

'So what are you doing?'

'Sunbathing on the veranda.'

Sun warmth shining through slits in the wooden planks. Planks that block us from the green alleyway that leads to the park. The alleyway that Josh could walk down, and peek through the slits and see me. Eye pressed against the wood. Me viewed through a vertical light strip. Light sight, blinking eye, me in a fence frame, lying in my bikini.

I get strips of sun and blob-shaped leaf shimmers that move over my skin. I'm at home and everyone is at school. I am meant to be sick. A day off, because we planned it. A day off and I'll ring you. And he has.

'In my bikini!' I giggle.

'Really?'

'Really.'

Lying where he could walk past and peek through. I stretch my legs. Stretch out in the sun and think. Think about him walking past and seeing me.

The first time we kissed was playing 'Dare, Truth, Promise or Command'. We had to be locked in Sarah's room. The room was summer white. I could feel the skintightness of my togs and the sticky saltiness of my skin. Swimming pool sun-dried skin. His hands never dared to go up. Up to feel the smoothness of breasts under pink swimming-tog material. He loved me too much. He was afraid of me.

Waiting in the park on Guy Fawkes night. Darkness was hours away, hours away but promising something sweet like tractor-mowed park grass. Grass that we were rolling down the hill on. Tumbling together. And then I was dared to kiss Karl Day. Karl whom I didn't even like. It was gross. My stomach hurt with the silence inside me. With Josh there was a beautiful silence; it was all the unsaid things. Things said with our bodies. Eyes that looked away then looked again. Eyes that sought each other out every morning, lunch and afternoon school break.

The smell of rockets. Writing 'Alexis 4 Josh' in the air with a sparkler.

Nobody to see that unless you let them.

'Alexis 4 Josh'. 'Alexis 4 Josh' written slow-quick with my sparkler. Quiet standing in the dark. Writing slow and fast, slow circles and fast lines.

Josh came and stood right beside me. I did quick scribbles.

And he wrote 'I love Alexis' real quick, but slow enough for me to know.

Good for a Laugh

Trudi Cameron

On the first day we met, you came to our house and filled the living room in that way of yours. Even the budgies weren't immune. Twittering in your honour. Later, I tried to teach them your name. My lips eagerly formed the syllables, as any fear of being caught adding to their vocabulary stayed hidden. I wanted to forget that I couldn't be seen to be keen, while remembering how you'd complimented me on my hair band. Even reached to finger it. My sister Lara scowled. You know how she does that?

Your proposal, in front of the family, was released into the air. It replaced the oxygen. Drowning, I gasped. Like pollen, it stung my eyes. Open wide, in spite of themselves, their lids powerless to defend. The tears were of joy. Of course. So unexpected. Welcoming you to the clan was a much privately practised act of my father's, and he did all right on the night. Later, our fingers touched, briefly, as they met on the salt shaker. Your raggedy man-hands made the shaker's silver pale into ugliness.

During the ceremony, nerves ate me. I tried to beam you in, mind to mind. Willing you to meet my gaze as I stood beside Lara. The lack of response made me think you were angry. I imagined it was because I wore apricot instead of white. At the reception, we got the chance to tango and rumba. Your special wedding shoes squashed my toes. I begged them to ache, urged them to turn blue in memory of the infliction, so I could admire the tangibility of my injury during the honeymoon.

When the time came to warm the house, I baked treats especially. We passed them around. Together. The ceramic platters had been wedding presents. You agreed that it was pleasing to see them being put to good use. I knew exactly what they cost.

When the baby was born, I was surprised when you said she looked a lot like me. All I could see was her father's mouth. Of course Lara was there, wearing my face with green eyes. The ones that should have been mine. She'd had a hard day, so she slept and left us to 'coochy-coo' alone.

One time, in the car, baby on my lap, I used anecdotes to entertain all. Your laughter rose louder than their worth. You turned to me in the back and said 'to the stage with you'. Now even Lara was amused. Hysteria-fuelled, together you presented a study of 'Mirth in Unison'. It became the fist that had me see stars. Or was it light?

At the engagement party of a very kind man, in the bosom of the home I'd help the two of you warm, Lara made the treats, while I made the jokes. Being 'always good for a laugh', I had no choice. Between receiving congratulations and a ceramic platter of my own, I managed to trigger many a snigger, chuckle, giggle and guffaw; until – for some reason – I told the one about my sister's husband's lover; about how he doesn't love her back. That one's not that funny.

Emily's Dahlias

Catherine Mair

Emily dug the skull up with the dormant dahlia tubers. It wasn't a grim-looking skull. In fact it looked almost cheerful. She left it lying on the dark soil and ran inside.

'Nina,' she yelled, 'Nina, guess what I've found under the golden dahlia.'

Nina said, 'Come on, Emily, what? A tooth? A wedding ring?'

Nina had come to live with Emily when Dick took off. Dick had cursed Emily and said that women like you two deserve a knuckle sandwich, or much worse.

'Phew,' said Emily when Dick left home and hearth in a spray of gravel. Later she raked smooth the doughnut he'd made on the drive.

The letter arrived a couple of days after Nina moved in. It was composed of letters cut out of a newspaper. Emily suspected Dick. The letter forecast dire events. It said that every time the women kissed they would get cold sores. Every time they touched they would suffer itchy rashes. Every time they smiled at one another a monarch butterfly would die. Nina particularly liked the monarch butterflies. To test the threat Nina smiled radiantly at Emily just as a beautiful butterfly hovered nearby. It dropped through the air and landed like an autumn leaf at her feet.

Emily and Nina had read about men who issued contracts to kill their wives, but this was a new twist. Sorcery. Here was something medieval. What could they do? Fight fire with fire? Pour chilli sauce on the flames? Then Emily remembered the skull. After brushing the soil from the framework of fused bones she placed it carefully in the middle of the lawn. She covered it with a cloth until Nina and she had sorted out their plan.

Nina was an expert seamstress and together the women designed two outfits. A beautiful monarch butterfly costume for Nina and a welcome swallow dress-up for Emily. When the women had zipped and velcroed themselves into their suits and wings, they turned up the music and began to dance around the uncovered skull. As they danced more and more giddily, they chanted, 'Diadems drop and Doges surrender, soundless as dots on a disc of snow. Dance, Dick, now.'

Ten kilometres away dour Dick began to feel an odd tingling in his feet. He had to get up. He had to turn on the music. He had to do something wildly joyful, unlike anything he'd ever done in his life. His skin turned a vivid yellow before it turned scarlet. He had to dance on and off as if his life depended on it.

Collapsing onto the mint-scented grass Nina imagined gaps left by fallen trees where huge butterflies drifted in columns of sunlight. Emily just wanted to sleep.

Man Alone

Jerry Chunn

Life, mused Mr Brumley, had often proffered the poisoned chalice to his lips, but seldom had he been tendered a second round with such indecent haste as on this balmy spring afternoon when he shanked two successive balls into the trees to let the C Grade Championship slip from his overlapped grip.

It had taken a long shower and several gins for him to detect a certain symbolism in the debacle. They had been the last of a dozen fluorescent balls his wife had given him for his sixtieth birthday. It had taken him eight months to lose them. They had, in fact, lasted no longer than his wife, who had deserted him for an orthodontist who claimed to be able to tap dance.

She remained for him just a remote presence, like a storm that had passed over and was now dampening the spirits of another province. Some day she would return with her Herod of a lawyer to cut their paintings down the middle and leave him with a bagful of memories.

Until then he had his exercycle, his list of resolutions, his wavering conviction that somewhere out there he would find a new start. At sixty? Grimly he argued that it had been done. There was Thomas Hardy and poetry. But when did he begin? Well, nothing really begins at sixty, he announced to the motorway traffic, it just starts again, gets dusted off, comes in from the wings. The thigh that came in from the cold – an old dinner party joke that had come, like most of his jokes, to bore him. He was running out of dinner parties anyway. Beware, my lord, of booze, he warned the traffic cop who sped past him. He had put that at the top of the last list he'd pinned up in the kitchen. 'Things to beware of: booze, going to the movies alone in his old raincoat, draughts, insolvency, love.' Now he would add 'shanking'. He had made it home. The traffic cop had failed again.

Shanking was due to standing too close? Too far away? He poured another gin and looked up *Easier Golf*. Too far away, it said. And losing a wife? Too close? Too far away?

All his records looked old and dated. They reminded him of twenty, thirty years ago, when he danced, when they all danced, and he'd been nimble of foot. Of course they did. Damn it, he'd bought them then, on Friday nights when they kept popping up regularly, all his old friends: Frank, Bing, Nat, Ella, Louis, Sarah. He had mixed large jugs of martini to zonk the guests as they arrived, and put on the latest, and they'd said, 'You've got a new Nat.' And he'd end up dancing with a drunken grace with someone, not expecting the song to go on for twenty, thirty years, outlasting Nat, the house, his marriage, his children growing up, even dancing itself. Perhaps not that; he'd heard it was coming back – 'touch dancing' they called it. Too late for that now.

He put on a Nat record anyway, and fossicked in the refrigerator. Could he have bacon and eggs twice in one day? Nobody would know. But it had to stop. He wrote 'Cooking' at the bottom of his list, under a heading 'Things to Learn'.

Dramatis Personae

Janette Sinclair

Miss Keegan, English lit teacher, was directing the fourth group in *Juno and the Paycock*. 'A powerful play,' she insisted at rehearsals, adopting a trace of brogue.

Secretly they laughed at her – her slash of lipstick hectic red as the people's flag, frantically flapping, her graduate's gown faded to the musty green of blackboards smeared with chalk-dust. But her dedication kept their interest. She brought in a varnished spinning-wheel (hand-crafted in Ashburton) and a shawl (an heirloom from Miss Keegan's Galway grandmother) which was handed over with some misgivings to 'Mrs Madigan' – Chrissie was an incorrigible gum-chewer, probably smoked on the sly. However Barry did the blustering jocular 'Joxer' to perfection, Hazel matured into a voluptuous 'Juno', and even Grant (who skipped several rehearsals for the pleasures of video arcades) gave 'The Mobilizer' a menacing conviction.

And if Miss Keegan privately nursed an ancient grievance that English literature rests a great deal upon the work of the Irish, she never harped upon it. But she always seemed to pick Irish plays for school drama night.

First the audience was taken through *The Mandarin's Hat*, a brittle farce rendered at breakneck speed, breathlessly and sometimes inaudibly, by the third form group directed by Mr Anicich, who was also a stage manager.

Behind the curtains Miss Keegan stirred her cast into an Irish broth. 'Well, your audience has had comedy, if they could catch the lines …' (Mr Anicich, passing with props, shot her a sour look. He had inherited from his Presbyterian mother a dislike of self-pitying

Irish, despite the Balkan ring to his name and the robust reds from his father's vineyard.) 'Now their mood is ripe for tragedy.'

The curtains parted again. Miss Keegan peered anxiously from the wings, prompt pages in hand. But those young people did a splendid job. At last the bereaved mother's keening filled the hall: 'Blessed Virgin, where were you when me darlin' son was riddled with bullets, when me darlin' son was riddled with bullets?'

From the wings opposite Miss Keegan a black cat stalked out. The audience quivered in sudden attentiveness; heads lifting, eyes unglazing, pointing, whispering. The cat wandered around, its tail brushing the dresses of the exiting 'Juno' and 'Mary', and arrived front-stage just as the drunken 'Captain Boyle' and 'Joxer' delivered their final lines on the state of Ireland.

Laughter billowed and bellied, drowned only by dutiful clapping when Miss Keegan, glaring desperately, raised her arms and signalled for the curtains to fall.

Now was it sheer accident, or the trick of some pesky leprechaun, or simply that Mr Anicich was a little tired of doing all the pulling of levers, clambering up ladders, risking life and limb on the school hall's shoddy wiring? But the curtains rose again and that cat took the encore; sitting back on his haunches in the footlights' glare, lifting a leg, lowering his head to clean a puckered pink star that shone out of black fur.

He Lies Down

Geoff Allen

The man in the doorway drinks in the innocence of his sleeping children. Behind him the hallway's harsh light keeps at bay the terrors of their imagination, like wolves at the edge of the firelight.

The man's threatening shadow, as if too tired to get up, twists over the strewn knickers and sweatshirts. In the arrow-thin light through the hinge crack the two cherub-like faces of the little brothers shine. Their faces remind him of the night-lit windows of the local church – a sanctuary he hasn't entered since his own uncomprehending baptism, but one he must trudge past each day on his way to and from work.

He turns the spare key between his forefinger and thumb. The metal filings stuck under his cracked fingernails glitter. His sons believed he was a god who bent iron with his bare hands. How long, he wonders, before they realise he's just a machinist. He longs to stroke the soft cheeks of his children, but his hands need scrubbing and even then he would still feel unclean daring to touch such straightforward souls.

He had it once – that time when dreams still danced around him and he could so easily touch them. When there was no difference between running through the bush flapping your arms and real flight. When Dad had been in a real war and he let you polish his medals once every year, and men who fought like his father were heroes.

Deliberately untying his blackened work-boots he places them quietly in the hallway. Just an hour, he tells himself. The man stretches out, his head nearly touching the base of the fish-tank. Inside which Roger and Camille swim in figure eights losing their memory every five seconds, falling in love again 720 times an hour. Maybe that's what we need, he thinks, losing memory.

He lies down, an old redwood crashing silently in the forest. He lies down to sleep next to his children, drawing in the same air for one night. Sharing the same moment in time; but not the same dreams.

Daddy, what if someone takes us in the night?

They won't.

But what if they do?

I'm here.

What if you're out?

Your mother's here.

What if?

Go to sleep.

But …

Sssssh.

Eyes unwilling to remain open he drifts into the past. The muscles of his face relaxing into sleep; becoming beautiful also. Just for an hour, he reminds himself. Otherwise they will jump over him in the morning. From him to the kitchen, excitedly spilling milk over their cereal, covering it with too much sugar. One minute jumping on you, the next hugging. Yet now he would gladly wake from any dream for either.

In one of his overall pockets is the non-molestation order. It says he is the wolf who sleeps by the fire.

Queen of the Night

Penelope Bieder

'Queen of the Night' is both the strange, night-scented plant under my parents' bedroom window and my father's idol, Rita Streich. Swathed in dark gold silk, she descends the staircase in *The Magic Flute*. From the circle, I look closely at her, and I don't like what I see.

Under the thick stage makeup and ornate head-dress, she looks just like Mrs Miller. I thought there were 12,000 miles between us, but here she is, shrieking her heart out on a Viennese stage.

Joy Miller, head teacher, hardly resembled her name. She was a handsome, cruel woman, with strong forearms like raw lamb-shanks. You could always expect an alarming combination of blood-red lipstick, loud voice and nasty temper. I was small, skinny, a dark misfit with Bandaids holding my glasses together and a scratchy uniform I could barely keep under control. Even worse, I had a foreign-sounding name.

At eleven I was discovering grown-up books, and they were far more interesting than Mrs Miller's classes. Learning about irony, love, malice and loss was so much better than sewing and cooking.

The small, rural private school was claustrophobic. There were only two teachers – Mrs M and Miss Dorothea Sawyer, a downtrodden old goat with grey plaits encircling her small, bony head. Cairnbrae Preparatory was a school for the offspring of wealthy farming families, girls with heads piled with merino-blonde dry curls, girls with pink strainer posts for legs, girls with double-barrelled names, posh lisping voices and hope still in their hearts. I left when our family visited Europe during what would have been my final Cairnbrae year.

One day in geography class, Mrs M announced that along with

the other Eastern European states, Austria was now communist. I had not liked what I'd heard about Austria, but I wasn't going to take this.

'It isn't …' I said. 'It isn't communist.'

Rows of benign, blue eyes focused on me. Like a nervous flock of lambs contemplating the motionless sheep dog, the girls stared. Mrs M's chalk slipped across the blackboard, screeching an angry yellow line. The wind blew more acres of glaring, white clouds across the tall classroom windows. A seagull, breast feathers parted, strained to stay in the cold air above the lonely, naked oak tree.

The dreaded words were spoken: 'Stay behind after class'. Everyone turned to the front, disappointed, shoulders sagging. They knew I could be useful in class. Once again, though, I would not be allowed to shame Mrs M. And she would have another excuse to attempt another clumsy flirtation with my father.

The day after the opera we visited Mauthausen in the Danube valley, where my grandparents died. Years later, back in this safe, sun-drenched Pacific town, the mocking dream seldom returns; and anyway, I can almost understand it now.

In the dream, plump, fair and frightened schoolgirls are being herded into a grey courtyard by a uniformed Mrs M. She is screaming Mozart at the top of her voice and she looks awfully like Rita Streich.

Cynthia's Landmine Blue

Katie Henderson

Victor has given her his dead mother's name. A whisper-name like a
snake weaving through her father's cornfield. When Victor calls her,
it sounds like a spit.

Victor touches his thin lips to the line of her parting, hands her a
blank signed cheque and flies to Wellington.

'Victor is Your Saviour,' her mother writes. Her mother still
believes the Khmer Rouge is hiding in the corn.

Cynthia glances at the baby playing on the tiles and continues
turning the pages of the *Edmonds Cookery Book*, committing to
memory the recipes below Victor's ticks. She can hear the TV
repairman clicking in the lounge. Soon she will have to fill out
Victor's cheque. She's good with numbers.

Victor lets her out on Sundays to visit Jesus. Nine Sundays ago
the Baptist Church Fundraising Committee elected Cynthia treasurer
because of her trustworthiness and skill with figures. She is making
the books balance. It is only words that give her trouble.

She watches the baby crawl up the hallway and finds him
fingering the screwdrivers in the TV man's toolbox. The TV is spilt
on the carpet. Punishment for poor volume control; half-words
and garrotted sentences. Cynthia understands impediment. The
repairman solders a circuit. A wisp of white smoke spirals up and she
lifts the baby away from the smell. Victor's photos have been placed
on the coffee table.

'The camera never lies,' says Victor, but Cynthia knows about
decoys. The Family Photo. Here are her mother and the three
youngest children (Batdambang, 1998). If the photographer had
taken one step backwards, you would be able to see six-year-old

Kosal's new and beautiful Red Cross leg. If Kosal had taken one less step forward …

The Wedding Photo. Here is the Hotel Champs-Elysées (Phnom Penh, 1995). Victor in his journalist vest looking proud and bald. Soon-to-be-Cynthia inclines her head towards him and her mouth smiles for the *Cambodian Daily*.

The Mother Photo. Here is Cynthia-the-First with the unfortunate teeth (Auckland, 1993). No one can guess the breasts under her blouse do not exist.

So much is lost in translation.

Cynthia cannot stop her fingers darting to her own breasts. Perhaps, buried somewhere beneath her skin, a small hard lump is waiting to detonate.

She prays the baby's teeth will come in straight. She prays for the whole sentences of her mother's voice. She prays Victor won't be expecting a roast.

The TV repairman reaches for her. 'There's your problem. Capacitor.'

A tiny blue cylinder rests on her palm. With its four spikes it reminds her of tripwires but blue is the wrong colour. Her voice trembles, 'My husband. He did not leave cheque. You send bill?' He nods and puts the TV back together.

Cynthia pokes Victor's cheque into a soap-powder box at the back of the laundry cupboard. It settles amongst wads of Baptist money. She drops in the capacitor like a talisman. For protection.

When the baby is in his cot, she runs the shower. The water says Mao Sopheap, Mao Sopheap, Mao Sopheap like rain on corn leaves. She lets her name wash over her.

Bernie's Bird Trick

Frank Nerney

'Show us the bird trick, Bernie,' Ally said.

'What?'

'Show us the bird trick,' Ally shouted over the lawnmower next door.

'Naw, got things to do,' Bernie said.

'Aw go on, Bernie,' little Fred said.

Ally and Fred were sitting on a beer crate in what Bernie called his back yard, though the neighbours had other names for it — rubbish tip, scrap heap were some.

'Please,' Ally said, drawing the word out so it keened in the ears like a hungry mosquito.

'Yeah, go on,' Fred pleaded.

Bernie looked at them with pale eyes. The kids were all right. They didn't act funny the way some adults did, making jokes or remarks about his hair, his clothes or a funny smell. 'All right then, but just once,' he growled, mock reluctant.

Billy was on his perch in the house, trilling with pleasure because the sun was slanting warmly through the window into his cage. Billy was a Scotch fancy, bright yellow, slender, with high shoulders.
He stopped chirping when Bernie and the boys appeared, and edged nervously away on his perch.

The cage door opened and Bernie's giant hand swooped. Billy tried to flutter away but not quickly enough.Bernie stroked Billy's feathers then put Billy in his mouth, so that only his tiny feet and his tail were outside.

The boys danced with anticipation.

Bernie took a deep breath through his nose, paused for dramatic effect, then blew Billy out his mouth like a cork out of a bottle of fizzy wine.

Billy, finding himself flying backwards suddenly from a dark, warm place, was disorientated and fluttered wildly to get his bearings. He landed on a table near the window and started teasing his rumpled feathers back into shape.

Bernie looked intently at the boys. They were laughing so much they could barely stand. Bernie grinned, showing teeth like ruined buildings.

'Again, again,' little Fred cried, 'oh please, Bernie, do it again.'

Bernie moved quickly and scooped Billy off the table and put him back in his mouth. Billy's tail and claws looked like an exotic, ethnic decoration fixed to Bernie's lips.

Bernie filled his lungs again.

Next door Mr Wilberforce ran over a small pebble with his lawnmower. The stone flew like a bullet over the hedge, smashed a small hole in the window and hit Bernie on the Adam's apple just as he expelled Billy.

Billy flew backwards, got his bearings and found himself looking outside through the hole in the window. He squirmed through.

It's big out here, he thought. It smells different. I like it.

The boys ran around trying to catch him while Bernie ranted at Mr Wilberforce over the hedge, but Billy was enjoying his freedom too much to want to go back.

Billy had nearly three hours of liberty before Mr Wilberforce's cat caught him.

As Billy went into the cat's mouth he thought, Oh no, not again. But only for a second.

The Truckie

Maureen Langford

She called it simply 'Annie's'. 'It won't work,' they said. 'Truckies won't stop – not with that long hill ahead. Won't stop coming down, neither.'

But one did. He strode in, Goliath in worn jeans and blue checked Swanndri, at 6am when she was deep in scone dough, and ordered breakfast.

'Bacon, lots of it, crisp, two eggs. Tomatoes. Toast. No coffee – pot o' tea. Strong.'

He ate, with the newspaper, which he had plucked in mid-stride from its stand, propped between the sugar and sauce. Outside, his rig waited in the chill half-light, a gleaming juggernaut embellished with the name 'Footloose'.

She watched covertly as she assembled the ingredients. The first cup was downed in one draught, the second in two. She refilled the pot. He looked up. A strong-boned face, not handsome, but not displeasing. Blue eyes, fatigue shadowed, crinkled suddenly.

'Customers like classical music, do they?'

'I play it for myself, early. The customers get middle-of-the-road.'

'Who's that?'

'Schubert.'

'Uhuh.'

He paid, loped towards the door. 'Great breakfast.'

'Thanks. Spread the word.' The door closed on a raised fist, thumb extended.

He came Tuesdays, frequently her first customer. She began listening for his truck changing down, knowing it from the others. He wasn't much of a talker.

'Are you Annie?'

'That's me.'

'Doug. Short for Dougal. Who's that?'

'Chopin.'

'Uhuh.'

His plate acquired more rashers, another sausage. From leaning on the table reading, he leaned on the counter, dropping remarks amidst the bacon's hiss and crackle.

'Bad storm in Wellington, shook us about a bit.' And, 'Auckland … Jesus! Don't know how they live there. Best view of Auckland's in my rear mirror.'

She liked that, liked him leaning, watching, liked the timbre of his voice.

One morning he leaned there, fingers tapping. Left third finger bare, like hers. 'Mozart?'

She met his eyes, direct, unblinking. Blue, with yellow flecks. 'How …?'

'Bought a coupla tapes.' A self-mocking smile. 'Didn't lash out. One's Mozart – quite good on long stretches.'

Her silly hands began trembling. 'The other …?'

'Tchaikovsky. I play that when I've topped the Bombay Hills. Da-da-da-da-da-da-*dum-da-da*! Fits how I feel.'

She washed her hair Tuesdays, wore tiny gold earrings, discarded the navy smock for a tee-shirt and skirt. What are you doing? her brain asked icily. He's not your sort. He could be, her heart cried, he likes music … Get real! Her brain replied.

He lived in 'Paraparam. Para-para-umu. Kapiti Coast. My Dad's place. Bit rough round the edges, but it does me.'

In her lonely bed she wondered about riding high in the cab, about Paraparaumu, about a house needing paint.

One Tuesday he didn't come. Nor the next. She listened, watched, fretted. Two weeks became four, then six. Pride forbade her to ask the others.

See! her brain sneered. You fool! He's just another truckie. Footloose.

But she missed him, his frame against the counter, the resonance of his voice, his language. Summer waned, the poplars yellowing. She considered selling.

Unseasonably early frost bit, the cafe cold in the hill's shadow. Coaxing the woodburner, she didn't hear the gravel's crunch, only the screen door's protest. Beyond him the cab door hung open, the unmistakable music in the chill air. He grinned.

'Who's that?'

She could feel her stupid smile spreading, stretching forever.

'Mozart. Same as usual?'

'Yep. Same as usual.'

Beyond

Peter Bland

He was looking through the mind, body, spirit section of his local bookshop (a rather splendid place with easy chairs and a coffee shop) when he noticed a most intriguing scent, distant, evasive, faintly eastern (as most scents are) but – in essence – something 'other', something he'd never experienced before. For a moment he distrusted himself and suspected the misty trace of some particularly subtle perfume warming itself on a passing wrist. But he was alone, close to aliens and anchorites, with no girlish hand exploring those bookish depths.

Further possibilities quickly presented themselves – a new brand of coffee, a Turkish cigarette, a sudden breeze from the flower stall outside. None of these lived up to further examination. Was this then the whiff of something alien or angelic? A ghostly longing that had somehow found a gathering place? A secret scented message from outer space? Do they have scents 'out there' in those deserts between the stars? In a flurry of belief that the answers to his questions lay hidden within those religious shelves, he began to unload their wisdom, a book at a time. *Poems for the Pope, A Day with the Dalai Lama, Secrets of the Incas, Visitors from Outer Space* were quickly piled up on a firm foundation of Korans and Holy Bibles. He felt like a child again, kneeling happily among his building blocks. But behind a large hardback edition of *Isis Unveiled*, that faint scent disappeared, crowded out, he felt, by the sheer insistence of spiritual understanding that weighed down those slender shelves. It was immediately replaced by the crisp comfortable smell of new books and the odour of his own damp clothes. He had no regrets. That whiff of the unknown was wholly of its moment. He sensed that if its origins *could* have been better known, then they may well have turned out to be disturbingly matter-of-fact (like heat from the sun or the inevitability of oblivion). So it was back to the cappuccinos and the easy chairs, with an erotically illustrated volume of *The Song of Solomon* somehow left open on his lap. Shades of a post-war Sunday School and a disapproving vicar. Childhood intimations of close encounters with future perfumed unknowns.

Ruby Anniversary

Bernard Brown

My uncle Ned, after the first months of marriage, spent his off-duty driver hours down at the potting shed, regarding his chrysanths. Auntie Maud, who'd acquired him straight from the trenches and preferred him shell-shocked, very rarely went into the garden ('Not ever having been summoned,' she said, the day he died on their anniversary).

I got the job of going through his things left in the shed. Piles of the *National Geographic*, an old ration book, six halfpennies ('Fares, please'), his medals, two pairs of missing schoolgirls' shoes. And longhand copies of a poem that I didn't dare to read.

The Key

John Allison

I've always been susceptible to fine bones; but clavicles, especially women's clavicles, fascinate me.

Clavicles are those bones spreading from the throat, often prominently, commonly called collar-bones; but there's an appealing delicacy about the Latin word. Someone said I was associating it with 'clavichord', that exquisite-toned keyboard instrument in which metal tangents strike the strings. And it's true I thought Sophie's clavicles musical, as sculpture can be musical.

Checking a dictionary I discovered there really was a connection: clavicle, from the Latin *clavicula*, meaning 'small key', the diminutive of *clavis*, the root of clavichord.

However, despite this susceptibility, I've never been able to touch them. I react to the idea of touching the bony protuberances of the body as some people react to seeing blood. This has made my relationship to myself awkward enough; just pulling on or removing my socks is an ordeal.

This should have been a sign, when I saw her clavicles, that Sophie would prove a *noli-me-tangerine*. My furtive glances initially disconcerted her; perhaps she thought I was looking at her breasts. Once in love, though, this was not the problem.

Throughout our relationship, I was aware that she was admired by men. I was also aware that she enjoyed this, while remaining faithful. Then, one summer night at a dinner party Scott turned to me.

'You know, Richard, I believe Sophie is adored by every man here, including myself. She's really very beautiful.'

I took it as simple envy, even admiration for my taste. I sipped my wine and smiled. I didn't mind sharing the image of her beauty.

Scott glanced at her. 'D'you know what I love most about her, Richard? This sounds ridiculous, of course …' He wiped his mouth. 'But ever since I saw her, remember, that barbecue last summer …? Well,' he leaned forward, 'it's those collarbones of hers. I just can't help it, I'd give anything to be you, just for a moment, to touch them.' He stroked his wineglass. 'Imagine that, getting off on collar-bones,' he murmured. Then he laughed, holding up his glass. 'I think I've had a bit much to drink. Excuse me.'

He'd seen my reaction, but was drunk enough to be only slightly embarrassed. The conversation turned towards other things, and I regained my composure.

But as summer developed, I watched her at the beach, I watched her at barbecues, I watched her clavicles and suffered. I found myself suggesting she cover herself up – the sun and skin cancer of course. I watched Scott watching her. Some unnameable feeling was growing in me – which she found claustrophobic.

Now I have the picture, and she has Scott. I sometimes think about this. She a *noli-me-tangerine*? I've seen them on the beach, he massaging sunblock into her neck and shoulders, and now I know. It wasn't anger, no, nor jealousy I'd experienced at his disclosure. It was horror. Disgust. Scott had felt pleasure even at the thought of touching – *touching!* – her clavicles.

Diamonds are Green

Laurie Mantell

Detective Sergeant Harcourt first met Brenda Lacey and her uncle Matthew Dryden when he was called to the chief's office that day.

Dryden handed him a ring set with a green translucent stone, saying, 'My niece had her engagement ring stolen last night and this was left in its place.'

A burglary, thought Harcourt. Something uniform could handle. So why him? He examined the ring closely then looked over at Brenda. 'Unusual. Burglars take things. Don't substitute as a rule. An emerald? And your ring is?

'Diamond.' She said with a catch in her voice. 'The Westlake diamond.'

Harcourt stiffened. The Westlake diamond was worth a packet. Now it was an emerald. He stared at Brenda in disbelief. For months he had been searching for the imbecile who had taken radium from Comstock Research lab. Now this.

'An emerald this size could be worth more than a diamond,' he suggested.

'Emerald!' she said in disgust. 'I prefer the Westlake. That's why I was so careful. Kept it in my bedroom safe. And this morning it was gone. Blair will be furious.'

'Blair is your fiancé?'

The chief butted in. 'Dr Blair Westlake. You know him?'

'Yes. I know Dr Westlake.' Everybody did. He had been attached to one of the government research labs until he inherited his uncle's millions. Then he did the sensible thing, resigning and setting up his own lab for private research.

'You have notified Dr Westlake, I presume.'

'Yes,' Brenda said, half crying.

Harcourt was saved from comment by the sudden arrival of Westlake himself. He did not seem too pleased about their little gathering. He went over to Brenda and grabbed her by the shoulders.

'The ring!' he almost shouted. 'You said it was stolen.'

Before he could say anything more, Harcourt held up the ring. 'Have a look at this, Dr Westlake.'

He did so and was visibly shaken. 'Oh, my God! Not that! Not that!'

'Your risk, Dr Westlake,' said Harcourt dryly. 'You see, Miss Lacey, diamonds exposed to radium turn green. Not a lasting effect but an old trick con men used to pass diamonds off as emeralds. I presume you have been holding a package for Dr Westlake in your safe. Unfortunately the lead container must've been damaged, because it's leaking. Recently we've been investigating the loss of some radium from the Comstock lab, and as soon as I saw your ring I guessed where it was.'

The Panda Family

Jan Marsh

I thought the knock at the door was the taxi-driver. How could he expect me to be ready when he was half an hour early? But I opened the door to two women.

The older one said, 'We visit people in love to bring a message of hope. The world is full of anger and aggression. Don't you long for a world of peace and love?'

She deftly opened a pamphlet to show me an improbably golden-skinned family in front of a high-roofed American barn. They were dressed in the styles of the fifties, pink dresses, checked shirts. The children were playing with two pandas, which seemed to have emerged from nearby trees and which looked oddly black and white in the gold glow of the scene.

The two women were nodding and smiling as if I'd just won tickets to the place. They seemed oblivious to large suitcases on the veranda or the fact that at 11 in the morning I was in my bathrobe. I said, 'I'm sorry but I've got a plane to catch,' snatched the pamphlet and shut the door on them.

I felt bad, but they had God on their side. I looked at the picture of the happy yellow family and burst into tears.

I wiped my eyes on the towelling sleeve and went to find the photo book. There was my paradise – Claire at the beach, her red curls sharp against the blue sea. I remembered taking the photo as she posed and laughed for me. That night we went out in the dinghy to watch the moon rise. As it came up huge and golden I leaned forward to kiss Claire and saw in the water a shape outlined in stars. She grasped my hand and we watched silently as a dolphin gleaming with phosphorescence slid under the boat. We sat for a long time holding hands and rocking on the dark sea.

I slipped the photo into my wallet.

It was kids that split us up. When I came out in my twenties I knew lesbians didn't have children. I grieved then accepted the fact. But times changed. Claire got very keen on babies – she even had a donor lined up. Well, she's younger than me. I told her it didn't seem right and no way did I want babies at this stage. She didn't argue, in fact she didn't say much for a long time. Then I learned about Josie and started packing …

In the end the taxi was late and I still wasn't ready. I'd torn up three notes. 'How do I leave thee? Let me count the clichés.' She'd see I'd gone, would probably guess where. Would she phone? I felt sick at the thought.

I left her the pamphlet of the improbable family. I identified with the pandas.

Out on the road the taxi horn sounded again. I took up my suitcases and walked.

That Summer, the Longing Summer

Kiyohiro Ejima

A winter land

It's a kind of sad day today, she's just left the country in the north for warmer weather, to catch another summer.

You'll be missing her very much the next two or three weeks, then it will be well into winter. The snow will fall, it will put everything under a big white blanket, and more snow will fall on top of that. It will fill the gaps between the mountains, the forests, the rivers, the fields, the villages; it will fill the gaps between the houses, the roofs, the doors, the walls and the windows.

The snow will fill the gaps in your mind too, and it will make some shapes, the shapes of her body, her face, the shape of her being. You'll pick them up gently with your fingers and put them in a small drawer of your chest. Every time you think about her, you'll open this drawer and know she is there; you won't feel lonely through the long, cold, dark winter until next summer, until she comes back.

A girl

'Where is your mother?' the voice said.

   'I have no mother, who are you?' the girl replied.

   'You must be lonely. Where are your sisters?' the voice said.

   'Where are you? I have no sisters. Who are you?' the girl asked.

   'You must be lonely,' the voice echoed.

   'I'm not lonely,' the girl said.

   'I'm not lonely,' the girl whispered.

   'I'm not lonely, who are you? Where are you?'

   The voice had gone. The girl was again alone, in the dark.

A summer garden

One day you'll see her walking up the narrow pass from the beach to your house. She'll be wearing a big creamy white hat, holding its top with her left hand so the wind can't take it away from her; the wind will make her long red hair wave and shine instead.

Within a moment you'll remember all, the hat, her hair, her hands, her body and her face. You'll start running towards her and she'll see your approach; she'll put her arms wide open to catch you, and you'll jump into her big smile with a push of an off-shore breeze on your back.

Your hugs and her kisses will turn the two of you into an ancient statue at the edge of your garden on the cliff that looks down on the vast ocean, the wind won't miss the opportunity to steal her hat away, far and high up over the water towards the sun.

You'll have been waiting a long, long time for this day.

You'll shout to yourself in your mind, She's here! Summer's back!

And this time …, you'll wish to the sky above her head.

This time …, you'll wish to the waves below her toes.

This time …, you'll wish to the wind caressing her cheeks, … it will be the endless summer.

The Butterfly Orchid

Virginia Fenton

I have a new granddaughter, born two weeks ago in San Francisco. She has my eyes, I'm told. They're sending the photographs. They called to tell me the day they were posted and when they arrive I'll be able to see with my own eyes that she has mine. They like to do this with every new grandchild. I've noticed it is a kind of ritual my children, my daughters and sons-in-law all have in common. It is what they mention after the assurances of vigorous health and good appetite. They tell me she or he has my eyes or nose, my ears even, my lips and the shape of my mouth.

I wonder who has my teeth and which grandchild has inherited which internal organ. Who has my heart, for example? Does someone have my spleen? Where have my lungs got to? I only hope no one will inherit my knees. Wouldn't you pity the child who ends up with an old woman's knees? It would ruin the heartfelt ambition of any grandson. They would all like to be famous for playing basketball. When they visit, I always tell them about a grandfather who was known locally for his physical strength and towering height. I don't know if this is accurate or simply a trick of memory, my least reliable organ.

I catch the train at Chungshan Middle School station and for a moment we travel above the traffic so quietly and smoothly it is like gliding. It almost feels like we are flying over the streets. Then the train rushes into the ground, as if the city has swallowed us once more, and I listen for my stop. I'll get off at Ta-an Forest Park. From there it is a short walk to the flower markets at Chienkuo South Road. I'm going to buy an orchid with petals like butterflies. I have already selected the shade of purple. I've chosen the flower and last night I moved the other plants in the living room to make a space for it. I have thought for some time about this visit to the markets and the flower I will buy.

If I could choose an inheritance for my granddaughter as easily, I would give her something similar to the butterfly orchid. It is associated not only with spirituality but with independence of thought. I would like her to have her own heart. I'd like to keep my tendency to worry. I'll keep my knees and spine and take them with me. Even born in a new country she will still have that mix of fortune that is her ancestry. I would like it to be true that she has my eyes so that this island looks familiar when she sees it for the first time. She will have a part of me. I would like to be able to choose which one.

Away with Words

David Hill

Martin knows that Brenda hasn't left the CD deliberately.

No – Brenda is all spontaneity, as in today's announcement that she's had enough pretending and she's moving to Cliff's to get her head together and think things out. Martin tries to imagine himself using words that way.

Words brought him Brenda. He dazzled her with them, netted her with books and language. Now that she's gone, the silence makes him stand still. Then he sees the CD.

Its lyrics have pecked at him ever since Brenda began crooning them that Saturday on the walkway:

> *Why don't we do it in the road?*
> *Nobody here is watching us;*
> *Why don't we do it in the road?*

Crooning, and fondling him as they walked. And when he pointed out how anyone might see, giggling too.

'So let them see. We are *married*, aren't we? Eh, Martin?'

After that, the CD or Brenda's crooning of it is a constant background. Martin plans another walkway stroll, but retreats before anticipated giggling.

Then Brenda goes to her brother's. Cliff of the cascading gut and 'GET IT HERE' t-shirts. She phones. 'We can talk on Sunday, eh? Bring my CDs over.'

On Sunday afternoon, halfway to Cliff's, he suddenly wants Brenda so hard that he grunts. Noise slaps him as he gets out of the car. People on the front lawn; music blaring through windows.

A man hails him. 'Lost something, mate?'

'I'm looking for Brenda. I've got some things for her.'

A bray. 'We've all got something for Brenda, mate!'

Titters. Brenda emerges, giggling, in a minimal sunfrock.

'You took your time. Bring those CDs?'

There is gin on her breath and perfume on her body. Martin hears his words blurt. 'I thought you wanted to talk to me. What's going on?'

'Oh, don't be so bloody boring! Here, Karla, put these on.' A chewing blonde takes the CDs and vanishes into the house.

'You said you wanted to talk to me.' Martin gestures at the sunfrock. Words … Words fail him. 'I'm disappointed in you.'

For a second Brenda's mouth trembles. Then her voice soars. 'Hey, listen, everyone! Martin's disappointed in me!'

Laughter spreads. Cliff looms.

'Isn't that bloody awesome? Hey, you wanna know how Martin disappoints *me*?'

Martin's voice is unreal. 'Brenda? I can't talk to you in this … brothel!'

Inside, someone turns off the stereo. 'This brothel!' ricochets around the silence.

Cliff's meaty hand drives into Martin's shoulder. 'Little prick! Insulting my friends!' The hand slams again. Martin staggers across the footpath.

'I came to see my wife!' Martin's eyes blur. 'Not this brothel and these slags!'

Cliff's fist crashes into Martin's temple. He's down in the gutter. His head jars on the concrete.

A foot swings into him. 'Little poof!'

Martin thinks the booming is inside his head. Then he recognises the words roaring through the living room window:

> *Why don't we do it in the road?*
> *Nobody here is watching us;*
> *Why don't we do it in the road?*

Wai

Phil Kawana

Wai sat on the edge of the veranda as the last of the twilight faded into the sea. The yellow light that spilled from the windows behind her became stronger, the patterns it cast on the lawn more definite, despite being distorted by the uneven fall of the ground. From up here on the hill she could see for miles during the day. But now, all along the coast, the land had tumbled into the darkness.

Overhead was a scattering of stars and a sliver of moon as thin as a child's fingernail. By the river, faint ellipses of light were dipping and diving amongst the trees. From time to time they flickered into crumpled cones, eclipsed by the macrocarpa that stood watch beside the road. There was no birdsong, no chirruping of cicadas, no rumble of motors or hiss of tyres. The only sound was the distant susurration of voices. Occasionally the breeze swept them deeper into the night.

She checked the phone again, making sure the battery hadn't run flat. Even though the indicator read fully charged, Wai wasn't reassured. She looked at it for several seconds, willing it to ring.

She took it with her as she stood and walked slowly towards the gate. As she slipped into the shadows of the garden, the lights along the river seemed to burn a little brighter. She thought she could see some movement down there, perhaps a flash of colour as someone scrambled amongst the gorse. Wai strained to make out who it could be, but the light drifted further along the bank before she could be sure of anything.

She was about to turn back to the house when she heard movement in the front paddock. There was a rustle, and a low snort. One of the steers, she thought. Wai held her breath and listened harder. In the meagre light, she thought she could see some of the herd moving reluctantly aside.

'Who's there?' she called, her voice cracked and dry like driftwood.

'It's me, Wai.'

Wai fumbled at the gate, and ran towards the voice, stumbling on the uneven surface. The phone fell silently from her hands onto the grass strip. Above her the stars faltered, fading in and out of the sky as she moved. She would've fallen, if Uncle Ngaru hadn't slipped out of the darkness and steadied her. Wai could smell the sea in the dampness of his Swanndri. He slipped something into her hand.

Wai had just enough time to recognise the small, saturated shoe before Uncle Ngaru's arms engulfed her. As he held her close, Wai could taste his salty tears.

Equality

Kathryn Simmonds

So I put the card up and they came – mostly from the state houses, the ones we saw go up when we were choosing names and going hand in hand on Saturdays to fit the decoration to our lives; we used to shop a lot in those days, moving between stores with magazines to match a colour or a print. One by one they came, faces slack with drudgery or taut with rouge. I smiled and poured them tea, watching as their blunt-nailed fingers closed around the fine bones of my china cups, noticing their eyes take little sips around the room, dipping from the paintings to my wedding ring.

They sat as carefully as debutantes, nodding as I explained the duties of the job, the weekly hours and rate. And when I'd covered everything, I motioned to the photograph of Christopher, the one that we'd had taken on his sixteenth birthday, seven weeks before. Briefly I described to them his handicap, as I knew I must, for fear his tendency to shout and fit was more than they could bear. I heard my voice come steadily, as practised as a doctor's, while I rested on the portrait in its solid frame. And as I spoke, the details of that day returned, the warmth of the small studio, the other unfamiliar families all staring down at us like happy witnesses. Side by side we watched the young photographer at work, struggling to arrange our awkward son into a pose, repeating 'that's it Chris, that's it', while we smiled on to show how it was done. Then at last the flash that caught the restless puzzled smile. Sixteen years, each moment frozen in one photograph.

As they left I shook their hands again, absorbing their shy pity, and afterwards I sank into the deep wedges of the sofa, listening to them treading back across the gravel drive. I followed them all day, as the shadows spread across the hills, reopening the doors that held their lives. I watched them move about inside cramped kitchens, switching on a kettle or a radio. I saw them in the evening, portioning meals onto cheap plates.

Later, taking little interest in the make believe of other people's lives, I felt them glancing at their children's faces, soft before the television set. I knew they would feel calm then, reassured, knowing that to clean another woman's home can not be hardship when it pays for school trips and new running shoes and the other things that buy equality.

Mickey

Janis Freegard

'Would you like to see my tattoo? I've just had it done.'

I'm in my favourite bookshop, a refugee from the wind on a wintry day. I look up from the book I'm lost in. It's a collection of Diane Arbus photographs: the ordinary grotesqueness of humanity. I enjoy slipping into her world. But it's a long way from the vision in front of me.

Never seen her before, but I'm glad I have now. She's so beautiful I can hardly bear it: translucent skin, red dreadlocks, ring through her left eyebrow, sea-grey eyes you could drown in.

'Sure,' I say. I would love to see her tattoo. When I'm not gliding through Diane Arbus books, I can sometimes be caught looking at pictures of tattoos. It's a fascination of mine. But then books are generally. One day I'll have a bookcase that spans a whole wall. I'll group my books by jacket colour and arrange them according to height – smallest on the left; tallest on the right. Red books on the top shelf; blues and purples nearest the floor. I will make a book rainbow, a fine work of literature and art.

I don't mind my browsing being interrupted when the reason's this good. She pulls at the neck of her wheat-coloured hemp top, exposing her right shoulder. I see delicate whiskers, an elongated nose, beady eyes …

'Rat,' I say, surprised. 'Cool.' And it is. A tat that stands out in a sea of skulls, roses and Celtic armbands. Can't show her mine without unbuttoning my jeans so I don't offer. (It's not a rat). She pulls her top back over her shoulder. The rat disappears.

'It's a portrait of my pet, Mickey,' she volunteers.

I've kept axolotls, seahorses and lizards, but never a rat. Mammals seem like too much responsibility. I've put Diane Arbus down. Mickey's owner has my full attention. We move away from the table; it seems we're leaving the shop together.

'Mickey Rat,' I say out loud. I like it. I like her. I realise I know her rat's name but not hers. It seems mundane to ask. We step out into Cuba Street; we're walking in time.

I want to ask her how she would organise the books on a bookshelf that spans a whole wall. I want to meet Mickey. I want to know if she's had anything besides her eyebrow pierced.

Still in step, we reach Lucky's. There are more cafés than real people in Wellington. It amazes me that they all stay in business. (I do what I can.)

'Coffee?' I ask. (I will die right there in my black leather boots if she says no. I will die if she says yes.)

'I like lattes,' she tells me. And then she smiles and the sun breaks out over the sea in her eyes and I start to swim.

Vintage

Geoff Henshaw

I remember the morning was hot. The dew had burned off early, which made the Dalmatians eager to begin. They started us on the merlot with the grapes so fat and bursting after the long summer that the juice leaked as soon as you touched them, turning your hands purple and sticky with sugars.

It was my first harvest. I'd hitched up from the Hawke's Bay with a shearer named Charlie who was going back to his wife and kid on the Kaipara. I was looking to get work in the city but he told me about the grape harvest out west and how he knew a place that would definitely take me on if I wanted. He said he was feeling so damned fine he'd drop me off there directly. I looked at him with his elbow out the window and his eyes on the road that would take him back to his wife and I thought how damned fine that seemed. 'Sure,' I said, 'why not.'

After the merlot we moved on to the malbec, which were black, more thickly skinned and easier to pick. It was then that I saw her, on her knees in the next row. With black hair and long fingers and sweat spreading down the front of her blue shirt. It wasn't yet Easter but she looked like Mary kneeling there in the morning light, full of song and God's favour. She smiled when she saw me. I waited for her at the end of the row with a ladle of cool water. She took it without looking. 'My name is Jack,' I said. She looked at me and wiped her mouth.

We spent the rest of the summer together, working on vineyards and swimming at the west coast's black-sand beaches, drunk on the fearlessness of love and youth. After we married I buried a bottle of that vintage atop Lion Rock. Call it a charm or something. But it worked — some days real hard when we felt the strain of meagre living and more than a few times I was ready to smash it and walk away.

But we've had something in our favour because it's been fifty years to the day. And although we still fight over whose life it is, who gets to tell it and where the damned thing is heading, tonight I'm going to surprise her. I'm going back to the Rock to dig up the wine and we're going to get a little drunk, because fifty years is a hell of a chunk of a time to be alive, let alone in love. But I don't need that Samson love that fades when the wine runs out, so say a prayer if you know any. And as long as you're down there, say a prayer for yourself. But you can be sure that whatever you ask for, we were given fifty years ago.

And it sticks like black sand to wet skin.

The Greenest Car in New Zealand

Frank Fell

Not just any car, but her husband's red Beetle, abandoned in the back
yard when he left. Shove by shovel she filled it with horse-shit and
straw, with worms that began to congregate like lost souls holding a
Mass for themselves, for the days of horse transport, and all the
wreckers-yard marriages left to stand in muddy paddocks – rainbow
puddles where the oil drips through.

Slowly the car took on new shape: a burial mound of autumn-
coloured rust, a cathedral, a Brunelleschi dome where the worms
burrowed through brake linings, transmission, clutch, upholstery –
name your car parts, the worms were there working in winter sun,
the horse-dung hot as an incubator that hatched a green iridescent
stubble, as though a balding man had struck it lucky with Propecia's
latest genetic engineering.

Call it a hobby, if you like, the kind that drizzles into your life on
a grey weekend, when clouds are slumped across the hills like a
judge's wig. Call it what you will – I watched her knuckles tighten
to white on her shovel as I helped her bury the car.

But as I worked beside her I'd find I was thinking of him: I'd hear
myself confronting him. I'd want to be saying that his old relic was
now a work of art, a living sculpture, the greenest car in New
Zealand.

I'd love to have told him that. But it wouldn't have been true.

It was nothing like that at all.

And he knew it.

Lunch

Adrienne Koreman

Jay has come to visit and I have made couscous. Piled up in a bright bowl, light and fluffy like newly hatched chicks. Each grain separate, but touching, with a slight fragrance of lemon and dashes of Italian parsley.

Couscous makes me cry. It was the one dish I could create to complement your marvellous Tunisian lamb, which you quickly fried in olive oil, your deft hand tossing in a spoonful or two of chilli paste and garlic, till it lay glistening in a pool of translucent red. Lastly, you'd throw in some roughly chopped spring onion and with one stir, there it was; an optical feast of fiery scarlet and tropical green on a delicate bed of the soft yellow of baby chickens.

'Lunch', you called it. Tunisian lamb, couscous, bread and red wine. Spicy and heady red wine. You would finish the bottle, and I would sleep with you in our warm summer afternoon.

And now, there is just the couscous. The soft plump grains waiting for the lamb to melt into them and drizzle through them and coat and cover them till they become one. A singular succulent spectacular sensation. Salty tears come, and they, instead, fall into the waiting softness.

We tasted each other's tears once and decided that meant we were bound forever, both ways, backwards and forwards as time goes; or around, until we come again to this moment in another life.

I spoon some onto Jay's plate. Will we too be bound, I wonder. But Jay doesn't have a memory of lunch on warm summer afternoons.

Airport

Vivienne Shakespear

She had become an old person, giving lengthy interviews to bored telephone pollsters, writing letters to the editor, imagining herself on first-name terms with talk-back hosts: 'Oh, you're not wrong there, Phil.' The words sounded like someone else's, which was a comfort; she had no desire to be odd.

While Phil picked a fight, she attacked her dishes. Dishes had become the trail of her days, the spoor she would leave behind should she disappear without a trace. ('Ah, cereal, not twelve hours old.') Of course, by the time the police arrived the cereal might be a week old or even a month and have a whole extra life of its own, but that was not a path of thought she chose to take.

(By then the radio batteries would be long dead and Phil's baiting lost to history. Everything in the flat could be fitted into two suitcases and sent down to her daughter, who would throw most of it away.)

The thought of all that silence made her cold. She turned on the heater. Yes, human voices were the thing, even if they did run away with themselves at times. Soft music got depressing, especially at night, as though it were being played to ease someone's distress. She did not need that kind of phoney sympathy. The place for that kind of music was the airport, where she went for a treat sometimes, sitting with a cup of coffee beside a young and radiant Jean Batten, forever poised for her first solo flight.

She loved the airport. It was like a separate city filled with a nervousness and excitement, and the music became part of it and was quite nice when you didn't have to listen to it. She loved the way people clung to one another as though they had been unintentionally separated for years, or were flying away, never to see one another again. She loved the smells of foreign clothes, duty-free shops, 'airport' air.

She loved the foreign babies, all swaddled up, and the little Asian children in their bright colours, like something out of a catalogue. She couldn't quite agree with some of Phil's callers when it came to Asians, even if they could remember the war. She liked the cooking smells coming out of council flats these days, and the strange words flung like handfuls of spicy seeds to children playing on the greasy grass below.

She liked the way the mothers smiled at her at bus stops, and there wasn't the same pressure as if they had spoken the same language and she'd had to think of something to say. These days it was quite hard to think of what might interest a person – a woman, say, of her daughter's age, with two teenage daughters of her own and some sort of husband. A woman like that was hard to talk to and would turn her stony face to the road and be deaf until the bus arrived, however long that might take.

Spa

Sarah Weir

The chips and dip go into a tail spin when we turn the bubbles up. Rosalie's famous floating serving tray bobs from one set of grasping fingers to another.

'Careful,' shrieks Rosalie. Missi reluctantly turns the jets down and leans her head back to gaze at the stars.

'Too many hairs in your mouth, if you ask me,' Chantelle says, continuing the conversation, 'like a chewy piece of gristle, I just refuse flat out.'

'I like it,' Missi says dreamily. 'All that power turns me on.' She edges closer to the jetstream until it shoots up her back.

'I think it's a bit like vacuuming,' Rosalie giggles, 'bit of a chore, but the end result is worth it.'

'What end result,' Chantelle snaps. 'A pile of French onion dip in your mouth. No way Jose.'

'No …,' Rosalie laughs shyly, 'I mean, then he … well … you know …'

'Lucky you,' Chantelle snorts. It's hard to imagine, looking at her hardened body, the nipples small beads screwed tightly on to a tough sinewy surface, her face pinched like it's facing a hundred-mile-an-hour wind, that anyone could get close enough to give her anything, even a slap on the back. She's just not the receiving type.

Rosalie wades through the water, refilling our glasses. Missi's thighs refract from below the water, air bubbles clinging to each black hair like fish roe. I want to kiss them all and I'm so drunk I'm in danger of telling them. These spa parties are a killer, I tell you.

Missi shrieks at Rosalie's coyness, and Chantelle emits a harsh, dried out laugh because laughing is the only way she gets a kick out of sex.

The French doors swing open and in walks Vern, wearing one of his fluffy lime green jumpers, a watering can in his hand. He stares at us, the piles of clothes, the empty bottles of Lindauer littered around the spa. Vern has one of those rubbery faces that gives the vague impression of being once inhabited by a woman, one who'd grown tired of being there and gone again. Stumbling towards us, with his wild, grey sideways frizz, he looks alarmed.

'I forgot you girls were here,' he says hovering, and for a moment I think he's going to sit down. He has to stay a moment to prove he's not shocked or embarrassed by us.

'So what are you girls talking about?'

After a brief silence, Rosalie says lightly, 'Oh, you know, the usual … knitting and stuff.'

We look at each other, a smirk bouncing around the pool like an echo. As he turns towards the door, I can't help giving his crotch the once over, imagining Rosalie doing her chores with frenetic energy, replicating the immaculate job she does on her carpets. He sneaks us one final glance and I sense him shrivelling, knowing damn well he's just been stripped, quartered and hung out to dry.

Walking Backwards

Patricia Lawson

The end of his scarf, his unbuttoned coat, the cuffs of his trousers and even his hair fluttered in tufts.

'It's too cold,' she called, 'come home.'

He looked at her painted fingernails clutching his sleeve. They reminded him of cherries, and sucking the sweet pulp and pursing his mouth to a sphincter so the stone slid through his lips to hit the neck of the girl on the ladder opposite him. He laughed and the wind caught in his throat and he coughed.

She clasped his elbow, steering him onto the path. She felt his bones through his sleeve. He'd gone off without breakfast. His impulses took him like a leaf in the wind.

Maggie's toe-nails too were like a bracelet of cherries through the thongs of her sandals, and his feet ripped each other as he'd swooped in the 'Palais Glide', and her skirt swirled above her red shoes and her hair webbed his face as they swayed. He laughed again and fumbled for his handkerchief to wipe his eyes.

'Have a rest,' she said. 'There's no rush.'

Silly old coot. He did everything at the double and then suddenly lost the plot and dozed.

She linked her arm through his.

'Slow down, Grandad,' she said. 'We'll take a breather.'

'Not so fast,' Maggie had said, 'there's my frock to be made and the church and everything.'

Her eyes were like the sky and the smell of her skin made his lips quiver.

'For ever and ever,' she'd said.

She coaxed him to a bench and looked over the sea. He'd taken her fishing when she was a child and piggy-backed her through the waves to keep her feet dry. If she was still here in the summer she'd swim again, though it wouldn't be the same without the kids thronging the bay. She looked at him under her lids. Away with the fairies.

And Mollie McGilveray had slid from the sea like a seal and the sand had coated their bodies and rimed their lips. He still found her here if he came on his own; heard her voice whispering like the waves slipping up the shore.

'You won't forget me,' she'd said. And he never brushed the sand from his feet without remembering.

There was soup to be heated and she could practise if she settled him in his chair and pocketed the keys. What went on in his head? It must be so dreary. All washed up and waiting. She squeezed his hand.

Like the red jelly beans he'd kept in his pocket for Sarah, or was it Janet – the first daughter with wild hair, like a pony. Sarah had been drowned when that bloody ferry foundered and Cathy …? Who was Cathy? He smelt pine-needles.

'Cathy …,' he said as he tugged her sleeve.

'Are you remembering Grandmother?' She buttoned up his coat.

Not a grandmother. He saw Cathy dancing the Highland Fling. He laughed.

'I haven't got a grandmother. Have you?'

Ghouls Will Be Ghouls

Linda Burgess

Julie phones Felicity to keep her up to date with what's happening with her daughter Georgie, who's having a baby. As she dials she closes her eyes and thinks, if she says that bit again about babies having babies, I'll …

Babies having babies! says Fliss, but so nicely you really can't mind, thinks Julie, not when she's so … well, lovely really, about Georgie, saying how all that stuff is nothing these days, nothing, and you couldn't be in a better place than National Women's. The tech*nology* there is *terrific*, says Fliss.

As long as they don't do another of their unfortunate experiments, not on my daughter, anyway, says Julie, and it's good to end the conversation with a laugh. It's good for you, a laugh. She does feel better after talking to Fliss. Always does.

Felicity is straight back on the phone, dialling Pam. It's not gossip, it's the network, and people do need to know, for the support network. Backup. In case.

She tells Pam that Georgie's got – what do they call it now? Something that sounds like a medieval instrument of torture, what we used to call toxaemia, says Felicity.

Oh Jesus, Fliss, what's the *prognosis*? says Pam, but Felicity says, truly, it's quite straightforward, they're inducing the baby; if some gel or other doesn't work they hook her onto a drip and if worst comes to worst they'll do a caesar, not that they're anticipating that. Or anything. Georgie was fine, truly. The baby's fine. She's fine. All will be fine.

We knew her at playcentre, says Pam. And now *this*.

She'll be *fine*, says Fliss.

Angela says to Brian that if he leaves his used dental floss by the bathroom basin again she'll fucking kill him. He hardly hears above the noise of the electric toothbrush, tinny little battery, but resolute. He likes to think of it dealing to ... Bertie Germ, that's what they used to call it. She's going on about Julie's daughter, some crisis or other. Reported to her by that ghastly little gossip, Pam. In the old days she'd have been strapped in a chair and dunked. Or even better, burned at the stake. Die, Bertie Germ, thinks Brian, giving the molar that has been causing him grief lately an extra buzz.

Bugger Brian, thinks Angela, self-absorbed arsehole. She'll ring Paula, who never cares what time you phone. Even if it is after eleven.

Felicity's stirring her porridge when Paula rings to say, My *gahd* did you hear that Georgie's having a *caesarean*?

Fliss says, No no, Julie has phoned, only minutes ago, baby was born this morning, all well. A completely natural birth. A dear little girl, says Fliss. Everyone's just fine.

But, she adds kindly, the *amazing thing*. In the next bed, a Chinese woman with a baby boy told Georgie that she'd gone to China during her pregnancy and two ... soothsayers I suppose you'd call them – *two* – told her to abort the baby because the stars and stuff were wrong. Can you *believe* it?

What are they going to call him? says Paula, quite cheered up now. Adolf? Or Genghis?

Yes or No

Lisette de Jong

My new boyfriend has curly, dark hair and lovely blue-green eyes. He's quite tall and wears a suit to work. Sometimes I meet him afterwards, in a bar or a restaurant, with his workmates. He talks mostly with them, but I don't mind. He's gorgeous when he's laughing and he has his arm around me. I smile and feel like the luckiest girl at the table.

Justin. I call him Just. Just Just – ha ha. My friend Debbie said, 'As in *only*,' and I said, '*No*, as in *justice*.' Justice. It has such grandeur and status.

'Is that a bruise … did he hit you?'

'*No. No.* It was one of those hard creme eggs – we were playing and he threw it at me, but I moved so it got me in the eye. It's quite funny really, isn't it? Ha ha ha. Oh stop staring at me, it's just a bruise.'

He's not like the rest. He's very nice and considerate. He does the dishes and cooks and even puts the toilet seat down. He loves the kids at my daycare centre and thinks I'm really talented at my job. He wants to have lots of children one day. And he calls me. He likes to know what I'm doing after work.

'Do you want me to come over … yes or no?' he asks.

'Yes.'

Sometimes he doesn't – he gets caught up at work or goes out with his mates and he forgets or it's late. But he calls me a lot. And tells me he loves me.

We go dancing every Saturday night at The Hall. He loves to dance, once he's had a few beers. He twirls me around like we're a professional dance couple, like we're made to dance together. It feels very romantic. He won't leave until the very end. If I'm tired Justin will often grab another girl to keep on dancing. Justin's a lot of fun when he's dancing. He spins them around too and they laugh. He doesn't slow-dance with them, unless he's really drunk. He must forget who he's with sometimes.

I'm the girl he holds on to for the last slow song. When he's at the stumbling stage it's me he leans on. I think of the song *Stumblin' In* on our way home. I hold him up as we walk to the door. By this time he's very tired and gets grumpy really quickly, so I get him in to bed as soon as possible. I have a shower then climb in beside him. He's usually asleep and I cuddle up to him. When I close my eyes, my head is spinning slightly like I'm still dancing. I recall him dancing with other girls and think that's how we must look together.

'Do you love me … yes or no?'

'Yes.'

Unconditional love is a beautiful thing. I expect he'll ask me to marry him one day.

He'll say, 'So, Angeline, do you want to marry me … yes or no?'

And I won't know whether to laugh or cry.

Inner-City Room To Let

Bill Payne

One single room, $110 per week. Includes bed, mattress, and two perfectly good blankets. Does not include food, power or access to Internet.

Includes a downstairs flat full of unemployed morons originally from the small towns of New Zealand who think it's so *cooool* to live in the big city and forever play atonal anthems to their glorious youth while holding loud and irrelevant conversations in passionate, meaningful voices.

Includes a large, brown, smiling family across the way whose sole aim is producing children, all of whom grow to a gigantic size in a very short time and have friends and relatives over for confrontational and abusive games of touch football or play marathon bang-bang-bouncing basketball games among the inner-city traffic and the cars parked in the streets outside – vehicles that are regularly daubed with graffiti, broken into or vandalised at night.

Includes an Asian family in front with a possibly insane, rogue alcoholic uncle who reminds me of Peter Sellers in *The Party*; an unfortunate individual they loudly abuse each night as – ever protesting his innocence in a weaker and weaker voice – he reaches his required state of nirvana somewhere near the bottom of a cardboard box of wine.

Includes a businesswoman next door with a dog called Luke who's left tethered for fifteen hours a day and irritates the neighbourhood by furiously barking at every flying bird and (sic) passing wind. Also has a boyfriend who's often found unconscious drunk in her outdoor bathtub flower-bed after having been refused entry at some unforgivable hour of the morning following a fight that everyone within earshot was able to witness from the discomfiture of their wakeful bed. The same sweet paramour who, in a red-faced tantrum, reversed back and forth into the business woman's car one evening before disappearing in a cloud of burning rubber and almost running over a six-foot-three, twelve-year-old Samoan kid about to finesse a slam-dunk. The same character who, nonetheless, single-handedly stopped the house next door, and probably this house and the house on the other side, from burning down to death and ash when the pair of skinny junkies who lived for a time above him and his business-tart squeeze nodded off while smoking and set all their op-shop bedclothes on fire.

Includes garage bands, drains that clog, a deck that floods, paper-thin walls, intermittent pest control problems and a prying, suspicious landlord. Twenty-four/seven traffic, two-day parties, repeated gendarme-alerts and every type of noise pollution imaginable.

No partners, children, relatives or friends to stay overnight. Visiting hours must be kept to a minimum.

Advert placed by white, heavy-smoking, homophobic Peter Pan who recently decreed that a complaining wife on a veranda was more than any man could take.

Anzac

Elisabeth Liebert

George booked sick leave a week out from Anzac.

Geraldine Peace had only been in town for two months. She laughed. 'You're going to be sick next *Tuesday*? Planning on pneumonia?'

She wore black, bobbed hair and courageous lipstick, and people said she'd moved to Twizel because she was going out with the HR manager. George looked at her for a long time.

'I fought in Vietnam,' he said.

Winds from the north and the nor'west brought snow down from the mountains in spring, filling the rivers and spillways, but by October the tussock danced in the heat. Geraldine carried summer into the office in the sweeping hems of her frocks, in her hair and the down of her cheeks. Mark moved her into Accounts. George found her there when he went in for requisition forms.

'Like the bloody desert,' he said. 'Sucks your juices dry.'

Geraldine's eyes were ocean green. 'Been here long?'

'Sixteen years.'

Geraldine pinched her fingers as if she were afraid.

In January Geraldine and Mark flew up to Taupo for three weeks. George ladled Jellimeat onto cracked plates for her two cats and watered the lawn, where patches of brown blossomed like fairy rings. Geraldine came back brown, too. She wore man's shorts in the garden and her legs were thin. Over the summer the black leaked out of her hair. One Thursday she wore a bandanna across her forehead.

'Caught myself on the shower door,' she said when George asked, but at lunchtime she ate caesar salad at Hunters alone, and that weekend she hired a trailer and shifted out of Mark's place on Jollie Road.

The junior staff house next to George's had been empty for five years. When Geraldine lit the woodburner, the living room filled with smoke. George gave her a hand heaving furniture and afterwards, while her cats yowled and yowled in the laundry, he shouted her a pint at Hunters. She smelt of sun and musk, and her lips left small, red shells about the rim of the mug. George wanted to tell her she was beautiful, but she was younger than his married daughter in Johannesburg, so instead he told her about the leeches of Song Ca.

She remembered Anzac.

'Pneumonia again?' she teased. George laughed, although coming home he felt as if his insides had been caught in a geyser, and at the RSA next day he drank more whisky than anyone, to forget Geraldine's moth-wing cheeks and her emptied eyes.

She came looking for him at three, in her gardening shorts.

'You'll make yourself ill,' she said as if it mattered.

She walked him down the concrete steps into the sun. The houses hurt his eyes and a bank-holiday family, strolling home with ice creams, paused to watch him negotiate the gravel path.

'Drunk.' The woman had a Louisiana accent.

But in the car Geraldine reached across and gripped his arm with her summer hand, and George rode home like a Kaiser.

A Gothic Folly

David Eggleton

Marching out of the manse, tricked out in undertaker's duds, his black eyebrows as shaggy as Shetland ponies, his black beard bushy enough to conceal a colony of nesting gannets, the archaic deacon, rumbling and whistling, set forth to the cemetery with Gaelic on his breath. There was a squawk from a seagull nesting on the head of the statue of Robbie Burns. The settlement of Dunedin this early Sabbath morning was wreathed, nay draped, nay veiled, in the heaviest of heavy-bottomed fogs. It was a fog dense enough, opaque enough, deep enough, and accommodating enough to hide a whole cathedral in, but there was no cathedral – because that hadn't been built yet. Instead there were the sodden graves and the haunting.

Oh, the horror of the haunting; citizens had reported seeing an infernal glow roaming through the gloaming of the cemetery; and some, including old Mrs Maud McCutcheon, had sworn they'd heard the shrieks of the city fathers creakily turning in their graves in the dead of the night. Mind you, Mrs McCutcheon was regarded as slightly eccentric, her bonnet home to quite a few bees. But then, last evening, Cliff 'Deadly' Nightshade, a bard of the town who often wandered among the graves in search of the Voice of Inspiration, had knocked frantically at the deacon's door, saying how he'd fled from the gibbering yells rising out of the unhallowed darkness and run all the way to the manse to report it.

So now the deacon had come out to exercise the restless spirits of this haunted boneyard built high on a bush-clad hill overlooking the grey eminence of the city – this mouldering boneyard sunk in the sour, curdled light of the morning gloom, but not today at least lashed by southerly wind and rain.

Although ye never knew, thought the stern deacon, there's nae place like Otago yet for snowing in the middle o' summer, and he grimaced at the shrouded heavens, then raised his big leather-bound Bible, ready to confront any ghosts who might be out walking and lay them to rest. What he wasn't prepared for was the sight of a kea hopping down the steps of a tomb. From the shadowy niches of the tomb peered gargoyles, frozen in stone immobility.

The Thief's Journal

David Lyndon Brown

It was at the time that I discovered Genet that I first noticed hairs sprouting from my armpits. I denied the possibility of any connection. Suddenly I felt I was walking around in somebody else's body and somebody else was walking around in mine.

Each Friday evening I would catch the train into the city and make a circuit of the junk shops and second-hand stores. I often returned home empty-handed, my spending money still hot in my pocket, but one evening I struck a vein. My hand was guided over the racks to extract a perfect, gabardine overcoat, a pinstriped vest, a white silk scarf. And then I found *The Thief's Journal*. I slipped it into my pocket and, yellow with guilt, sidled from the shop.

In the cafeteria at the station, I examined the cover of the paperback. A melancholy face was superimposed upon a collage of Michelangelo's *David*, superimposed upon Bosch's *Garden of Earthly Desires*. I squinted through the blue smoke of my clandestine cigarette. With the change from my spree I had bought a packet of ten. Other than the odd puff after school, I had never smoked before, but the elegance of the new old clothes and the stolen book seemed to require an adult vice.

As I read, I felt as though I had been hijacked, suspended over a seething pit, lowered into a world I never suspected but recognised as surely as my own reflection. A netherworld of pimps and thieves, homosexuals and drag queens. I devoured the book in the sepia light of the train on the way home, where I hid it at the back of my wardrobe with the cigarettes, a half-smoked joint and a bottle of vermouth. Lying in bed, I could feel it radiating through the house and felt ashamed for infecting my parents' hard-earned air with the latest symptom of my degeneracy. The book's noxious rays would certainly lead my mother straight to it.

In the weekends my parents visited my grandmother in another town, and I was free to inspect myself in their full-length mirror, peeling off the new clothes until I got down to my new body. I took out the secret contents of my wardrobe and laid them out like sacraments in the lounge, which I had transformed into a Marseilles whorehouse.

I reread *The Thief's Journal* until it fell apart. I was unstrung by its delicate brutality and I realised that something crucial was happening to me. Something terrible and wonderful. And I knew that the change was irrevocable.

The growth in my armpits spread to my groin and filtered down to my legs. I shoplifted *Querelle of Brest* and *Our Lady of the Flowers* on my expeditions to the city and my solitary, decadent weekends soon escalated into noisy parties. My new friends brought beer and marijuana and stayed all night, and I spent every Sunday, before my parents returned, cleaning up, getting rid of the evidence.

Now You See Me. Now You Don't.

Jo White

I was once told that if you didn't believe in God, He couldn't see you. So I have spent most of my life dashing between belief and disbelief. Eyes open, eyes shut. Playing peek-a-boo with God.

His eyes were closed when I had my husband's name tattooed on my bottom at the Tattoo-On-You parlour in K Road and made love to the tattooist later. I kept my eyes open as the man undressed and revealed a delicate montage on his thin white body. And I hope He did not see me as I drank the tattooist's warm wine straight from the bottle. (Though whether it was the cheapness of the wine or the sex that I regretted more later on, I cannot say.)

His eyes were open when I visited my grandmother and helped find her teeth, then sorted her yellowing underwear from one mothballed drawer into another.

I am sure His eyes were shut tight each time I had sex with a stranger – although when I cried out 'Oh, my God' I suspect He may have peeked.

When I fed the neighbour's cat I sang childhood hymns to draw His attention to me. The cat was indifferent to my songs.

'Hello?' I called to Him, hoping His eyes were open. 'Hello, I'm here.' Hoping to be noticed. By the cat. By my husband. By God.

My eyes were open when Paul Holmes first started to talk to me from the television set. I am sure His eyes were shut when I caressed Paul's face through the cold crackle of the screen and held the remote control in a hot, wet clutch.

Then, as I stood in the queue of those waiting for book signings, I hoped His eyes were still busy elsewhere. For I'd accidentally prayed to be one of those lucky enough to get Paul's autograph.

As well as his signature I got a smile, so I offered to show him my tattoo.

'No thanks,' he declined politely and his eyes moved quickly onto the next supplicant, the next flyleaf.

'Hello,' I said desperately. 'Hello, Paul.' But his eyes were firmly averted.

When I confessed my sins on Sunday, in church, all went dark and I knew that He had decided to keep His eyes shut. Or was it that my eyes were screwed tight against His light? I do not know.

Now that He no longer looks at me I am free to do what I want. But the thrill of the game isn't the same when only one plays. And since I cannot believe that God has abandoned me too, I sometimes call His name out loud and try to catch Him peeking surreptitiously at me.

My husband hasn't commented on me squinting as I try to catch sight of Him from the corner of my eye. He doesn't see me as I cry over Paul's photo in the *TV Guide*, and he hasn't even noticed my tattoo, or the tooth-marks embossed on my inner thigh.

But then, he never looks at me anyway.

Gwen's 90th

Linda Gill

Judith said, 'I wish you could've found something else to give her.'

'Mum, we've been over this. I think it'll be a joke, and God knows we could use a laugh. And as I've said, this happens to be the busiest time of the year for me and there it was in the shop window on my way from the office. Just drop it, will you.'

Judith dropped it, but not out of her mind. Hot and angry, she stared ahead through the windscreen, cowed by the speed at which her daughter drove. Emma's impatient, clipped speech cowed her too. Dammit, she was entitled to a point of view on this, her own mother's ninetieth birthday. Emma's thoughtless gift was not going to add dignity to the old woman's nursing-home life.

Judith had fretted about her own present for her mother. And then she'd hit upon the idea of a book of photographs and for a month, utterly absorbed, almost entranced, she'd done nothing else. She went through all the old albums, choosing which of the family snaps to have copied and enlarged. She'd pored over the photos, her own life shifting to fit within the repetitive patterns of so many years passing by. Decade by decade she worked through her mother's life, easy to do in the early sepia years, but swamped with colourful choice over the last twenty. She bought an expensive hard-covered book from an art shop, and carefully glued the photos in, adding witty or heart-warming captions. Finally she'd made a beautiful title page with GWEN in gold lettering.

In the nursing-home, Gwen was sitting up in bed, wrapped in a mohair shawl, like a little bird in its nest.

'Happy birthday, Mum.' Judith bent over and kissed the thin skin. 'Here's your present, dear. Shall I unwrap it for you?'

Eagerly she tore away the pretty paper. 'There. This is your life, Gwen ... Tarum tarum ta *ta.*'

She began to turn the pages. 'Look, Mum, here you are in your christening robe, and here's your mother and father, and here ...'

'Yes, dear. Yes. How lovely. Perhaps later, dear.'

Gwen's eyes wandered distractedly to her granddaughter.

'Happy birthday, Gran. I bought you this.'

Emma pulled the teddy bear out of her bag, unwrapped, there'd been no time, and anyway the old lady couldn't handle wrapping paper so what was the point.

Gwen took the soft toy into her arms and stroked it. She held it up close to her face and peered into its brown glass eyes. She rubbed it gently against her cheek. Finally she tucked it into the bed beside her.

'There,' she said, 'my very own teddy. Now I won't be lonely any more.'

She looked up at her daughter and granddaughter and gave them a wholly cheerful smile.

Now This

Simon Reeve

It's strange the way you imagine things happening, and the way they actually do. Take Justine, the love of my life – that whole mess. It's over. She didn't stay with me, but she didn't go back to her husband either. I keep imagining I'll meet her and what we might say – she's changed her mind, I've changed my mind, we've grown up, it was a mistake, we can work it out. I imagine meeting the child I imagine is mine, saying tender fatherly things. What I don't think of, ever, is running into Grant, her husband.

I'm walking along the road towards the bakery, the lines arcing above with all that blazing electricity, the birds swooping down the shop-front corridor, ignoring the lights. I'm working nightshifts, it's my day off. Grant has ceased to exist for me, never peoples my mind; but there he is, standing on the footpath in front of me.

'Greg,' he says.

I look at him, my mind working slowly. Grant?

His fist is hard like walking into a door. I see it coming then it arrives. I step back to keep my balance. I'm surprised, startled. I was only going to say hello.

I wave an arm, shouting, 'If that's all you want, you can bugger off!'

Afterwards I reflect on the curiosities of it: shouting before fighting; using my father's language, not my own; imagining for some non-reason that I could simply say hello.

I put my hand to my mouth and find I'm bleeding. I wouldn't have said he hit me that hard. He stands there puffing like he wants to go at it some more, but like he's waiting, too – for me to start fighting back. I walk past him into the bakery, not listening when he starts yelling himself.

A man is at the counter being served. While she serves him, the lady can't stop looking at me. The man glances back then quickly looks away. He takes his change and disappears.

'A sally lunn, please,' I say.

She knows me, she serves me often enough, but she stares like I'm someone else. I take a tissue and hold it to my face. Instantly it's soaked with blood. I take another. She hands me the bag, I give her the right change.

Grant's gone when I step outside. I check, but can't see his truck anywhere – a beautiful old Ford, lovingly restored. Very distinctive. From now on, I start scanning the street for it.

I study my face in the mirror. The whole corner of my mouth hangs open, a badge for who I am, where I've been. I ought to go to the doctor, but I don't. I decide not to.

Let it heal how it heals.

Parting Shots

Alastair Agnew

The younger of the boys, feeling himself strangle slowly inside his Sunday clothes – predominantly a nylon torture – looked down from where his nose was, while the grandmother polished his shoes for him.

She was willing to do anything with her thick elbows to make the shoes shine – or if not, press the feet harder still into the dark floor, which was frequently dealt with in a similar fashion.

The boy's coat itched too, and he turned, twisting, inclined as he was to get away at the first chance.

His parents were upstairs getting the cases – which explained the polishing – and his brother, under solemn oath or deadly threat, had been sent as far as the front gate. To stand and wait and shout. When the taxi.

The youngest, listening to the brushing, could see his brother out there now, down the hall and through the open door, scratching at the brickwork with a stone or a stick. The younger boy was pinned beside the fireplace. He couldn't go yet. But soon. He was trapped where the poker. And the grandmother on both knees, her swishing now tending towards a praying motion.

Then he said, because he was still experimenting with cruelty and because of the sounds coming down the stairs, his parents bickering, the cases being dragged.

In this tiny moment.

'Might never see you again,' muttering loud enough for only the two of them. The tone was exclusive. Or inclusive in as far as the kitchen was concerned.

'Don't say that. Feet together.'

'Mum says. Never ever.'

'Your mother didn't say anything of the sort.'

The grandmother tapped at his ankles with the brush. But gentler than might have been anticipated. The boy wincing, ready to run. She was then getting slowly to her own feet.

The boy wriggled again inside his shirt. And loosened the collar button, suspecting with some confidence that no-one would care for the time being.

His parents were in the hall. Out past the front door the black mass of a taxi appeared in the gap beyond the gate.

It was obvious that they should go. The boy's father, counting himself fortunate not to suffer the deadly fate of inactivity, was arranging the transfer of the cases out over the curb and into the open boot of the taxi. The driver stood waiting.

'I saw the map.'

'Yes,' said his grandmother, who had too. She began slowly to pack the polishing kit with her otherwise unoccupied hands.

'We might not.'

'What?'

'Not see you again,' the boy persisted, but already growing bored with the experiment. Because despite the liquid expansion of his grandmother's eyes, she was pushing him firmly out to where the others. Who were ready around the taxi.

Only later, separated, would the two of them feel freed from these various constraints.

The grandmother in her chair by the kitchen table. Tea could only but go cold – milky questions forming on the still surface.

The boy in the taxi discreetly rubbing first one, then the other foot with the opposing extremity. Until the shoes he was wearing turned grubbier even than when he first put them on.

Moment of Truth

Jane Riley

Everyone's eyes turned towards her. She tried to smile but her lips got stuck to her gums, so she lowered her gaze and tried to imagine she was somewhere else. Somewhere warmer, somewhere infinitely more relaxing. She'd never done this before and was now wondering what on earth had made her do it. Was it Jim's subtle persuasion? Was it her inability to say no? Was it mere stupidity? She shuffled her feet and felt grit stick to her soles. They could have at least vacuumed for me, she thought, and almost began laughing at the ridiculousness of her desire. As if. The smell of chewed gum wafted towards her.

'Come on, Jen,' he'd said. 'Just to help me out. And it's good money too.'

'Aw, I dunno.'

'Yeah, you do. Come on, it won't be as bad as you think. They're not really going to be looking at you – not like that, anyway.'

'Yeah, right.'

'No, it's true.'

'Mmm.' She didn't believe him. But she did need the money, especially since she'd just walked out of the café after Josh had yet again pinched her bottom. She should have known better than to have stayed after the first time. But it had seemed harmless enough and she hadn't wanted to cause a scene. Except he kept doing it, and the pinches got harder and his smile dirtier. Jen shivered.

Suddenly she remembered where she was and rubbed her gum-tickled nose with the back of a hand. A bright sun appeared from behind clouds and pierced the windows opposite, making her yellowed toenails shine. Her feet felt cold and sticky and all she wanted to do was sit down.

Come on, Jen, you can do it.

'I think we're ready now.' It was Jim's voice from the back of the room. She looked up to see him smiling at her and nodding. She swallowed. Twenty wide-eyed students sat poised and waiting. Jim raised his eyebrows and nodded again. Jen drew in a deep breath and felt the paisley robe cling to her thighs, its flimsy weight the only thing protecting her from what was about to come. Fixing her eyes on the wall just above Jim's head, she began fiddling with the tie around her waist. As it undid, she felt the sides drop away to expose her firm rounded stomach. Taking another deep breath, she gently eased the robe off her shoulders and let it slip to the floor like a deflated parachute. She waited for the gasps but there weren't any. Her exposed skin tingled in the cool air and she wanted to look down to check that everything was still in its place but didn't dare. So she took up the pose Jim had shown her on arrival and temporarily stopped breathing as the students began to paint.

Sleepwalking over the Bumps

Gerry Webb

The lime was going on real good. Dry, talk about dry, the grass was so crisped the tyres were bedding into bare dirt, the big six purring like a sleeping cat and the blower was fair chucking the white stuff out, what with the reconditioned fins and the big westerly giving it an extra heave. There's nothing like chopping down to bottom cog and grinding up a shirt front with ten ton on behind, then coming straight down with just thin air below you.

I was doing the final strip along the ridge where we boundary with the hippie joker when who should come ploughing up the slope but the man himself. No mistaking the old Vanguard, he just had grey-green primer on it, made it look even more like a tank, except he had this hard-case canvas canopy on the back like a wagon out of the Wild West. But the funniest thing about it was the way it kind of sleepwalked over the bumps – stuffed front shocks I'd say.

Well, he leaps out and I could see right away he had a flea in his ear. Accuses me of drifting 245T down onto his place – nice little patch of dirt it is too, good flats, good water – and something about poisoning the planet with dioxin and plutonium or something. Well I just gave him a friendly pat on the back and ribbed him a bit about not knowing the difference between lime and hormone, but he was red hot about spray never drifting over his way. Fact is, we've *knocked* the gorse and now just fly 24D on for the thistles. Hormone is harmless anyway. Told him how we used to get under the hose to cool off when we were doing gorse with the tractor. *That* made his eyes stand out on stalks.

Somehow I got talking about our little Brethren church out at the coast and how I love it when it's my turn in the pulpit. I did a bit of a dummy sermon on Armageddon and how the Good Book is dead-on with its prophecies: you know, the mark of the Beast, 666, already on the supermarket bar codes. And Israel and the Middle East still the hot spot that could blow the big fuse any time. It's all about oil really, isn't it? But the hippie guy never stopped scowling, so I stopped and said, 'It's your turn, what do *you* think?'

'Absolute *crap*,' he said.

He fair spat it out and I tell you his eyes were literally flashing. Fiery little guy. I think it was Armageddon that rubbed him up the wrong way. He reckoned it was 'a cop out' and 'fundamentalist fatalism'. Sounds like a case of the runs, eh.

Strange little coot. I bear him no ill will though. These young people straight out of the city don't chew the fat like we do. And they're shockers when it comes to the weeds. But *they'll* find out if they stick around long enough.

Keeping Up with Hermione

Helen Mulgan

My friendship with Hermione started when we were both at school. It was an achievement just to have a friend called Hermione. I'm Joan.

Hermione was exciting and different. She had opinions about many things and did not accept them ready-made from her teachers. She was interested in art, but couldn't be bothered with our Art Appreciation classes where we looked with admiration on *The Blue Boy* and thought that *The Laughing Cavalier* was just a bit daring.

She told me that if I liked a picture at first sight, that proved it was superficial and dismissable. It didn't seem logical to me, but I usually thought what Hermione told me to think.

My first boy friends were drawn from my brother's football friends. Hermione did not approve. 'If men must kick a ball about in the mud, that is their affair, but they shouldn't make a public spectacle of themselves.'

When I did marry my favourite footballer, Hermione said we could still be friends and she gave us a significant piece of sculpture for a wedding present. But it's understood that we never talk about Super 12, when she visits.

Years ago she introduced me to her passion for Andy Warhol. She showed me a picture of rows and rows of baked bean cans. I felt betrayed because they looked nothing if not superficial.

'But don't you see, because they are simple, they throw back in our faces the superficialities of contemporary culture and art.'

'Yes, Hermione.'

Then she tried me on a picture that was just rows of small pictures of Marilyn Monroe. It was like a sheet of extra big postage stamps.

'It's a good likeness,' I agreed, 'but wouldn't once have done?'

'No, Joan. Repeating the picture so often underlines the sameness of the way Monroe was presented to the world.'

Okay. I'd try to adjust.

When I redecorated my home, I looked forward to showing it off to Hermione. But as soon as she entered the room, it seemed to lose its fresh prettiness and become obvious, like a showroom at Farmers.

However, she kindly ignored my co-ordinated colours, but pounced on my goldfish bowl on the sideboard – a pleasant touch of whimsy, I thought.

'That bowl is a metaphor for you, Joan. Can't you see that it represents constricted circles. No reaching out. Think about it. It's so confining.'

'I like it. It underlines the restful sameness of my life.'

'Not at all. I don't know how you can sit down and eat your favourite salmon fillets and look at all that coloured fish flesh wagging around in front of you.'

The fish had to go. The bowl is a wormery in the garden now. I think that's okay aesthetically.

I suppose you're wondering why I'm sitting here talking to you from a wheelchair. It seems that the thinking woman now does step aerobics to ward off osteoporosis.

I never could keep in step.

A Slight Change in the Weather

Raewyn Alexander

Ordinary days may hide startling events. Ordinary does not mean dreary. It means plain, everyday, routine, the kind of thing you're used to and often quite like.

There's a tight, dry feeling to this day, though. Let's not damp down anything. Two weeks of windless, sunny weather and nights raucous with crickets had desiccated Bob. He imagined being confetti floating in a breeze of good wishes. Taking his time to do anything in case the heat made mistakes, Bob found the time to be observant.

On his stool at the news-stand, he was invisible. People were used to his dumpy figure waiting for payment. They ignored his plain shirt and brown trousers and cloth cap while they made a selection. Regulars asked how he was, but in that way when you know people always expect the same answer. Lately, for fun, Bob sometimes said, 'Much better thank you,' or 'Getting over it.'

This elicited puzzled stares or further enquiries, which he brushed aside with a laugh. Some regulars muttered, 'Good, good.'

Then strode off with their paper or magazine as usual. The heat made Bob cantankerous, annoyed at being treated like a fixture.

'The plan is,' Bob told his cat while spooning out a good helping of Mature Mog for the ancient animal, 'to start small. Just a touch of something new, to see what's what and what's not. A bit of a laugh.'

Fresh touches were hidden for the first weeks, silk underwear, then a pedicure, visits to the gym and every morning a gargle with good mouthwash. Bob sat straighter and had a gleam in his eye, feeling not unlike a teasing fish, just below the water in sight of the angler, but nowhere near the hook.

His hair became a work of art over months – longer, swept up, mousse: a rinse to bring out auburn highlights that should have been there all along. He gave his cap to the Mission shop.

Clothes became Bob's fetish for weeks. Trousers in polished cotton, a see-through shirt over a mesh singlet, then hand-tooled boots. The morning he wore a silk lava-lava over his Capri pants and slipped on a heavy Italian jacket, Bob hummed to himself.

They say if you put a frog in cold water and heat it gently the animal will die without alarm. Customer's ideas of the news-stand man altered gradually. They readily accepted his flamboyance and charm because it melded into their days slowly.

The man's gentle hum became a quiet song until Bob stood tall one winter's day on his red-draped stool. Notes flew from his ruby Revlon mouth into the chilly air, a melody of love and betrayal that mesmerised commuters. The song's strength and beauty brought Mr. A. B. Hoffington's blue rinsed head around and his silk suited body to a halt.

Each night lately Bobby Blue arrives early, buys a paper from the news-stand and tips the weedy young man ten dollars. He's well paid for singing at Hoffie's Cabaret. Bobby always whispers to the news-stand boy, 'Best of luck, kid. Follow your dreams. You never know where this job will take you.'

The boy is pimply and sullen. He wants to fly to Russia and join the ballet. Escaping this concrete cage is a ridiculous idea, but each night he lifts just a fraction more from his seat.

Swans on the Water

Phillip Wilson

When Eileen went round to the back of the bach to see if Bob's brother was somewhere about, she got an awful shock to see a strange man with his arms flung out lying on his face in the long grass. She crouched down and tried to roll him over.

'Come and give us a hand, Bob. Looks like we've got a drunk on our section or something. Or else …'

She held the man's wrist, trying to feel his pulse. But there wasn't any reaction. Bob called out from where he was parking the car on the road.

'Who is it Eileen?'

'I can't tell.'

'Hang on a bit. I'll be with you in a minute.'

She didn't want to utter the horrified words that were on the tip of her tongue. If the man who seemed to be out cold was someone Bob didn't know, then a second question arose.

'What was he doing on our section anyway, Bob?'

She heard several large black swans calling on the river. They came cruising smoothly among patches of toitoi and tall bulrushes, attracted by the sound of her voice, remembering the tit-bits she usually threw to them when she was down here.

As she tossed her bits of bread on the water Bob came round and helped her to roll the man onto his back. She saw with foolish dismay that it was Uncle Eric.

'Eric! What's he doing here, Bob?'

Bob undid Eric's tie and shirt and put a hand on his heart.

'God, Eileen. Quick. He isn't breathing. Poor blighter.'

'What can have happened to him?'

'He must have tried to get into the bach, but had an attack and collapsed while trying to force the window open.'

'He's got a key, Bob.'

'Maybe he lost it.'

'Did you know he was coming? Or about his heart?'

But Bob didn't answer. Looking at Uncle's calm uplifted face she was thinking of past days now, and all the fun they'd had. Kindly Uncle Eric, his smallness, aloneness, physical deterioration, what Beckett called the Proustian equation of time, habit, need – Eric's split self talking to itself. She sensed it in his face, the absence of love or hope and the approaching end – habit, memory, need, desire, lost love.

'Poor old Eric. Come on, Bob. We can't stay here this time.'

The swans were approaching closer, persistent in their chattering. Their cries seemed to encircle her. The ominous sounds of swans flowed around them like some controlling power was directing her responses. She licked her lips and smiled as Bob hugged her, enjoying his warmth and the salty taste as tears of dismay and pity coursed down her cheeks. But a wheel kept turning in her head. A voice was quietly telling her to be up and doing, even if she was going to make a fool of herself, or she might never sleep well again.

'Yes, I'll go and phone the police,' Bob said.

Aunt Sylvia's Silver

Joy MacKenzie

I wasn't born with a silver spoon in my mouth so Aunt Sylvia sent me one, engraved with my name, *Janice*. My first memory (or so I like to believe) is the coolness of that soothing spoon against my angry red gums as I cut my first tooth. Aunt Sylvia sent me cutlery, a piece a year. It arrived on my birthday, wrapped in brown paper.

Spoon, fork, knife. In that order. I was capable of scraping blackberry jam from the jar before most children were entrusted with a knife. Auntie Sylvia was a spinster, with no experience of children. Who else would send a small girl a fork for her birthday? Not a doll, not even a book, but a silly old fork.

'She means well,' said my mother. A fork! My name looked good though. Attempting to imitate the fine handwriting, I covered the inside cover of *A Treasury of Nursery Rhymes* with *Janice*, paying particular attention to the loops in the J. What kind of spoon did the dish run away with? I knew. A tablespoon, of course. What did the Owl and the Pussycat eat with? A runcible spoon. I never got one of those.

By the time I was sixteen I had a four-piece silver table-setting. Then Aunt Sylvia broke the pattern. She got married to Mr James, watch repairer and engraver, and she sent me a soup ladle. I liked this. It was smooth, solid and elegant. We didn't go to the wedding. Invercargill was too far away.

Aunt Sylvia kept sending me cutlery and we sent soap and embroidered handkerchiefs. Also, thank you letters: *Thank you for the nice silver spoon you sent me for my birthday.* And photos. A photo for every milestone, because poor Aunt Sylvia didn't have any kids. *Janice winning the egg and spoon race.*

The day before my twenty-first birthday Aunt Sylvia choked on a corned beef sandwich and died. The knife arrived the same day, wrapped up in brown paper. So, by my coming-of-age I had a six place silver setting. We sent our condolences to the engraver.

Unlike Aunt Sylvia, I married the first person that asked me. Some time later, while browsing in a collectibles shop, I was startled by my younger self in a silver frame. *Janice at her first ball.*

'That's me,' I told the young man.

'No kidding.'

'Where did you get it?' I asked.

'Some old geezer brought in a box of stuff. Over there. Whole lots of knives and forks. No use to anyone. Unless your name's Janice.'

Needless to say, I bought Aunt Sylvia's cutlery. I also bought a fluted caddy spoon, six apostle spoons and a toddy ladle. Kiri Te Kanawa takes a few knives whenever she travels. If she wants to cut a slice of melon, she can. Aunt Sylvia taught me that there's something very dependable about cutlery.

Rosalie, RIP

Sheridan Keith

I think of her when I make meringues. She has attached herself to this process so that I can almost feel her hovering overhead as I crack the eggs. People like my meringues. I don't say this to boast, as there is little skill in making meringues. There are two tricks: the first is not to get the tiniest morsel of egg yolk in with the white; the second is to beat the egg whites like crazy and for much longer than you think you need to. Then, when they are climbing up the beaters trying to escape, then, and only then do you start adding the castor sugar. I was making meringues one day when Rosalie popped by, as she did in those days. She was trying to have babies without much luck. I had just had one and was wondering what had hit me. We would drink lots of green gunpowder tea, and grow silly. I was separating the yolks from the whites in my usual fashion, which is to crack the shell in half and fling the yolk from one half to the other, while the white sort of dribbles off down the shell, into the bowl. Rosalie watched me doing this and started roaring with laughter.

She had amazing brown eyes that were always alight with enthusiasm, but why was she laughing? It was my method of separating eggs. How else could you do it? She showed me. She cracked the entire egg into a bowl, and then, with her fingers, she plunged them into the egg and plucked out the yolk as if it were a floating island waiting to be lifted from the sea. It was bold, even outrageous. My technique she derided as fussy, mannered. But I didn't like her method one little bit. For a start it wasn't hygienic, and for another, it seemed far more prone to accident. Eggy yolks are fragile things, they don't necessarily hold together very well when you try to lift them out from the white. She conceded the lack of hygiene, but wouldn't change her ideas.

I am making meringues now, and although I remember the way her hand engulfed the egg yolk and held it triumphantly aloft like an eye removed from its socket, I stick to my fussy mannered way of passing the yolk between two half shells. But Rosalie, don't think I have forgotten you. I had moved away from London by the time you found out you had breast cancer; at least you had your baby, though a motherless child is not a happy thought. I don't have any profound ideas about our lives, your death. I only know that whenever I make meringues I think of you, and how we would laugh and watch the slithers of dust in the light coming through the big windows that looked out onto that road. There was an especially pleasing group of silver birch trees planted on the bank opposite.

Child's Play

Ro Cambridge

A skeletal, scab-covered dog snarled feebly as we climbed from the blissfully cool interior of the taxi into the blare of noonday sun. Palm trees drooped.

'Nice house,' said the driver, dragging our suitcases into the house that came with my husband's new job. The empty tiled foyer echoed like a public toilet. My husband tried the taps in the kitchen. They spurted gouts of rusty water. We had a two year contract, a bed, a television and nothing else until our own things arrived.

My husband began his new job. I bought plastic plates and knives and forks from the shop 300 sweaty metres down the simpang. Then I lay exhausted on the cool tiles watching television. A fan stirred soupy air.

Weeks passed. I waited to feel better, but by the time our packing cases arrived my torpor seemed permanent. Occasionally the phone surprised me by ringing, usually my husband checking on the current depth of my lethargy.

'Are you there?'

'Yes.'

'I can hardly hear you.'

'I'm here. Wish I wasn't.'

'What're you doing?'

'Nothing. We got those magazines back from Customs.' They lay gutted in a pile on the floor. Black pen obscured what little text had not been scissored. 'No sign of the books though.' How I'd ached to slap the avid hands of the ugly little customs officer who had confiscated my books and my carefully secreted bottle of whisky.

'What did you say? Hello? Hello?'

My husband came home for lunch. He tactfully skirted the stacked, unopened crates.

'I bought a padded jacket today,' he said.

'I think I need one too.'

'Not that kind. A quilted one.'

'What for?'

'The office air conditioning's on full blast and no bugger knows how to turn it off.'

My husband gave the fridge a pessimistic glance.

'Come upstairs.'

He attempted to make love to me on the ugly carved bed. I lay listlessly under him watching the fan spin in the ceiling.

'What are you thinking?' he whispered into my hair.

'The cat's got ticks.'

'Christ,' My husband slid off me.

The muezzin wailed from the mosque.

'When I pulled one out, this big piece of fur came out too. Oh. And I saw a monkey.'

'Where?'

'Out the back. It stared at me and then it went back into the jungle. I felt bloody lonely went it left.'

My husband was suddenly vertical.

'We're going out.'

The Chinese restaurant served whisky disguised as tea. We grew drunk pouring each other polite porcelain cupfuls from a blue and white teapot. Afterwards, we giggled our way through a nearby department store. My husband discovered a set of alphabet blocks. He tinkered with them a moment, then nudged me to look, 'FUCK IT,' the blocks said, neatly rearranged in their box.

Back home, we chanted 'Fuck it! Fuck it!' like a mantra, as we took up our cheap knives and levered open the packing crates.

The Epiphany of Sister Patrice

Frankie McMillan

'A book must be the axe for the frozen sea inside us,' quoted Sister Patrice. She kneeled to pull off my shoes. My toes were cold. She slid my slippers on and slapped the soles playfully. 'Do you agree?'

Two days later Sister Patrice stole a typewriter for me. It came from a downstairs ward and was an ugly black thing with a stiff plastic cover. 'God intends for you to write, Jamie,' she whispered. She whipped out the typewriter from under her blue habit and placed it on my locker. We both stared at the stolen offering. Sister Patrice looked down at her hands.

'I'm only thirty-eight,' she said.

I began my story the next day. I was the dying hero of course. And my girlfriend was the narrator.

In 1989 we had a runaway nun in the back of the van. She came bolting out of the hospice with a small battered suitcase. I thought she'd have a milk white face and a vulnerable neck. But she didn't. She wore blue track suit pants, a white cardy and a big crucifix. When we stopped at the lights she wound her crucifix tightly around her hand. We wanted to ask her questions. Like if she still believed in God and did she know about eftpos and how to find a flat, but Jamie had warned us not to ask.

'She's going through a spiritual upheaval,' he said. The way Jamie said it was like the road might suddenly erupt before us, might suddenly spew forth molten rock or rain down burning steam on the bonnet. So I didn't ask and Ollie just kept staring out the window.

The nun leaned over the front seat. A dusty odour like old sandals came from her.

'Thirty eight's not too old to begin again?'

It was hard to know where to go next after that line. And the typewriter was heavy on my knees even with the beanbag Sister Patrice gave me.

Next morning I took off on a new tangent.

Dead men's shoes. There they were piled on top of her desk again. Brown shoes, black shoes, tartan slippers with a broken zip, vinyl slip-ons curling up at the toes. They made a heap like decaying fish. How many times had she told the orderly. Label the shoes. Tie the laces. Put them on the Deceased shelf. Not all over my desk, dear God.

Down the stairs Sister Patrice began to run. Haltingly at first then she gathered her skirts. Her legs flashed white over the grass, and as she ran her blue veil billowed behind her like a snatch of the sea.

I can see those words. It could be a film. (Camera pans back to pale young man coughing into blood-flecked hanky. He keels over just as the last page is finished.)

But … maybe not.

So I begin a third story. Three is the number of transformation.

I think Sister Patrice would like that.

The Daisy Patch

Jeanette Galpin

Both the babies were dead. They had been born dead. Muriel has been called from her cottage in the August morning to deliver the roadman's wife; in her long skirt she runs across the paddock from one house to the other, her boots sink into the boggy hollows, to warm her hands she folds them tight against her armpits as she runs.

In the small cold bedroom she works all day to save the babies. The first is breech presented; the second pale and strangled by the umbilical cord. She wraps the tiny bodies in torn sheeting and lays them in a wooden butter box and taps the lid down. She throws the bloodied bedding into the kauri wash tubs.

The mother seems too exhausted by her ordeal to care much about the babies – she lies wrapped in blankets on the horsehair mattress with her eyes fixed on a far-off ceiling; the roadman's son has not been seen since he called on Muriel this morning with urgent applications on his way to school. The roadman has enlisted and it seems he might have left this country road for good.

Muriel washes her hands at the tap on the tank-stand then refills the kettle and stokes up the range and makes the roadman's wife a nice hot cup of tea …

The butter box with the babies is under the kitchen table. The shovel of the roadman is leaning against the tank-stand. A hurricane lamp is hanging from a nail. Enormous hills loom all around the little house; the light is fading and on every ridge the bush-burnt totara sentries hold their arms up in surrender. By the neglected gooseberries a soft patch of short grass is covered all over in white daisies.

Muriel is encompassed by a sort of ruthless fatalism. The shovel cuts easily through the yielding soil and as she digs down in the darkness the light from the lantern shafts upwards against her cheekbones. She smoothes the topsoil flat when she has finished and rests against the shovel; the weeping gullies and the sharp-cut chasms of the hills are all around her but she hardly sees them.

Only days ago it might have been since Mickey the postmaster walked round the road with the telegram in his hand. There seemed to be no sense or sequence in the handing over, no reason in the formal wording of regrets. That her eldest son had done his duty and lay dead now – somewhere in the stinking gullies of Gallipoli, after the dreadful farce of the Anzac landing.

She told herself she knew nothing of the loss of men to shot and shell, nothing of the screams of torment, the stench of bodies – nothing of any of this.

And yet – here behind the roadman's house among the daisies, sweating and exhausted and leaning on the shovel with bloodied hands from the thorn bush – here – after burying the babies, she thought she did know.

He Drove a Yellow Cortina

Jackie Mason

His jeans were a couple of inches too short in the legs. Could I go out with someone whose jeans weren't long enough? He seemed comfortable with himself. I had to look away.

I talked too much. He must have thought, 'God this woman's desperate.' It was just that I wanted to get him into bed. I found out that he was an earth sign like me, but not what date his birthday was.

He danced the way he wanted to. Could I go out with someone who danced like that?

He didn't ask me out. He arranged a date through a friend. We slept together.

I had to wait two weeks to see him again. He turned up unexpectedly. I didn't know what to say.

He worked in a tannery. We both liked chocolate.

His hair was fascinating, dark and wavy. When I made the bed there was a scattering of dandruff on the pillow. He said, 'It's only skin.'

His arms were long and warm. He wanted to hold me a lot.

I wouldn't let him go shopping with me because I don't go shopping with 'men'.

Whenever he went home, I would change the sheets, shake off the 'skin'. His leaving hurt. I was covering up the traces.

At his house I could hear the ocean. He played me music I had never heard before. It blew me away.

At times it became hard to breathe. Too much passion about everything.

I went back to school, to find myself. I had his baby. It was all very natural.

He moved in. He moved out. We didn't know how to live together, only how we felt. We grew apart. We grew together. So this was difference.

This Christmas he gave me music. I couldn't speak again. I remembered everything, especially passion.

He gave me life. He danced the way he wanted to.

Memories

Dorothy Black

Derelict and abandoned, the old house stood sheltered by the huge macrocarpa hedge against the ravages of winter. The glass in the windows was long gone, the gaping empty frames haphazardly boarded up, but now the doors sagged against what was left of the interior partitions. Remnants of the rusting roof flapped against the weathered rafters waiting for the next storm to sweep them away.

The old place was only fit for a bonfire. Anyone, even as prejudiced as the old man, could see that. But he could not bring himself to put a match to it. He much preferred to leave it still mouldering away until only the old hedge, planted when his grandfather was young, would be the reminder of the family's pioneering days.

Leaving the protection of the huge trees, he moved off to trudge through the rank grass. Running his fingers along the bleached weather boards, he felt the bite of a large hand-saw. In his mind's eye he could see his great grandfather standing above, the labourer below in the pit, dragging and pushing that heavy saw as they roughly fashioned the felled kauri trunk into this needed sheathing. Not much more than a hut to begin with, a lean-to was added, then two bedrooms on the front, and later a wing to accommodate the growing family. The cottage had become a home and it served two generations well.

Gradually progress over the years had widened the bridal track into a dirt track for bullock wagons, then a metal road for hard working farm traffic, and later more modern cars came as the main road bypassed the old home, leaving it stranded at the back of the property.

A new house, more imposing, was built nearer the road. The next generation moved in, and the old house was put to other uses. Labourers' accommodation or shearers' quarters, until finally it was reduced to nothing more than a hay barn.

The old man sighed, remembering those days. Many happy childhood hours he had spent playing in the sweet-smelling hay, hearing the scurry of field mice, the gnawing of water rats in the floor joints, or the twitter of sparrows nesting in the roof.

But haymaking methods changed. Subcontractors moved in to leave large canvassed rolls in the harvested paddocks for winter feed-outs and the old house was unwanted and forgotten.

Except by an old man and his memories.

The rattle of machinery broke into his reverie, returning him to the present. When he could ignore the noise no longer, he pulled himself together, crossed the paddock and strolled to meet the new arrivals. The time had come. There was no going back.

Taking a lingering look at the old place, he turned and waited for them to pull up beside him. There was nothing more he could do, and he greeted them reluctantly.

'It's all yours now,' he said. 'You can take it away.'

The demolition gang moved in.

Morning

Idoya Munn

He wakes in the morning and looks up. The sky above is dark grey, growing lighter. He was dreaming about something – what was it? Yes, they were walking through some bush, and a branch had scratched him in the eye. He went to rub it and found bits of bark and branch, they wouldn't come out. And when he looked up she'd gone.

In the shower he tries to wash the night off his face. His flannel is faded, rough. He holds it up and breathes in. It smells old, of sitting on the edge of the bath for too many days. He fights the wave of sleepiness and lifts his head. A crack has started to form in between the bath and the plastic sheeting. The water is seeping in there, guaranteed. The dampness collecting underneath will be rotting the floorboards. He mentally adds that to his list of things to do, some time. He steps gently out of the shower, minding his knee. He grabs the towel off the rail opposite. It's damp. He rubs quickly all over and then, with one hand on the wall, dries carefully between his toes. He starts to think about the day.

It's going to be rainy, says the radio. Showers expected across most of the isthmus, clearing late afternoon. He leans over the bench and pulls up the blind. There is nothing much to see. Dull grey sky over the concrete driveway and the neighbour's clothesline, tea towels and underwear flapping wearily.

Suddenly he remembers that in his dream he had been looking for a dog. A mutt with a broken paw, or something. It was funny-looking, its head twice the size of its tubby little legs. Dreams.

Lately he's been having a lot, just before he wakes, so that the faded memory lies under the surface of his consciousness for half the day. The other morning it was something ridiculous: he was sailing in his pyjamas and suddenly the mast snapped. Next thing his father was behind him bellowing in his ear, you can do it, son, just keep going.

He finds a bruised apple at the bottom of the fridge and puts it on the bench. He goes into his room and opens the cupboard. He takes a tie from the selection inside the door and stands in front of the mirror. He places it round his neck and evens it up. Then carefully right over left and under and then through and pull it tight until it's just so. He peers forward to double-check. He notices white flaking skin around his mouth and he leans closer. Suddenly he's staring into his own empty eyes.

He finds himself back on the bed, looking up. The sky is grey, darker in patches. He leans over and picks up the phone. I'm not feeling well, I'll be in later. He leaves the phone off the hook. He loosens his tie and closes his eyes. It all starts again.

Fanny's Stories

Jan Farr

That night Fanny wore a dead fox around her neck. 'Found it in a garage sale in Oslo,' she said. 'A real snip.'

Otherwise things were more or less as they always were when Fanny came to dinner. She arrived empty handed and consumed like a garbage truck. Her stories ballooned and fought for light and air until the walls creaked.

At midnight Ruth and Phil waited for her to breathe deeply enough to let them get a word in.

At two Phil touched her arm.

'Isn't this fun, pets?' she said. 'Let's crack another bottle of that nice red! It reminds me of the summer I spent in Siena. Did I ever tell you …'

At three Phil took off his tie. Ruth saw his nostril's flare and heard his warning sniff. She willed him to whack Fanny with the empty bottle and dump her body at sea. She thought then that Fanny's mud-coloured eyes had moved knowingly from hers to Phil's and back again.

'You must tell me about your new job, Phil!' Fanny cooed. 'Oh, and speaking of jobs! You'll never guess, kittens! Michael's asked me to work for him! You remember – the French art dealer with the big whatsit.'

Surely the house will pop, Ruth thought, as wine glowed again in the glasses and Fanny's stories puffed up to gargantuan proportions and the air grew too thin to breathe and the story of Phil's new job died on the worn carpet.

At three-thirty Fanny glanced at her watch. 'Good God, is that the time? You won't mind if I bunk down, will you chickens?'

She gurgled. 'Did you hear about the night I went to dinner with a sheikh in Brunei and got home three days later? "Just call me Sheherazade," I said …'

Again the stories swelled and the foundations groaned. Ruth felt sweat break out on the back of her neck. She swayed and clutched the table.

'Are you all right, darling?' Phil asked.

'I think Phil should take you back to town now, Fanny,' she said.

'What was that, my sweet?' Fanny stretched and yawned. 'I'm whacked! I'm not even going to bother you for a towel.'

Ruth felt the floor tilt. She stumbled to the kitchen, shut the door and leaned against it. When the rocking beneath her feet stopped she ran hot water over the neatly piled dishes. 'Bitch!' she hissed. She squirted detergent noisily. 'Me, me, me, me, me, me, me, ME!'

When the last dish was dry she went back to the sitting room. Phil sat in front of the fire and watched television. He raised his glass. 'The two of us,' he said.

'Where is she?' Ruth asked.

'Snoring.'

Slowly, Phil lifted his eyes to the ceiling. Ruth's followed. The fox – Phil's tie knotted around its neck – swung from a beam.

'He left a note,' Phil said. ' "Homesick for the Fjords." Tragic really. I got to him too late – not a thing I could do!'

Brain

Victoria Frame

Crystal doesn't suit her name. At least, she doesn't think she does. Fragile, transparent, delicate. None of which she is.

Crystal enjoys taking the balls of lint out of the washing machine. She scoops them out gleefully, savouring the sodden weightiness of them beneath her fingers. She is positive that if she opened up her head, her brain would consist of matter such as this; grey – the by-product of something significant.

'The mind boggles,' is her uncle's favourite saying.

'The mind boggles,' he ejaculates with alarming frequency and force.

'The mind boggles,' he muses, stroking his curly beard.

Crystal imagines a large grey brain looking deceptively like a fly's egg beneath a microscope, bulging, boggling, pulsating. A giant wad of wet, soggy lint, taking on a life of its own.

Sometimes when she lies in bed at night she thinks she can smell her brain boggling, boiling in her head. It smells like liver frying in a pan. It makes her feel sick.

'Did you leave your brain at home this morning?' her teacher asks sarcastically on daydreaming afternoons. Crystal jumps at the sharp tone of his voice, and looks up, horrified. Her brain is sitting on the pillow and expanding and contracting with a rhythmical beat. It is pleased with itself for having escaped from her head. Smug, almost.

There is a new phrase that the teachers are using at Crystal's school – 'brainstorming'. 'Split into groups and have a brainstorm about this or that topic,' they say with self-satisfaction, as if they themselves have invented this catch-phrase. Crystal doesn't join a group. Instead she looks down at her desk hoping no one will notice if her brain does not join in with the storming. She shudders at the thought of her brain joining forces with like-minded matter to form a collective grey mass. She does not want to give her brain any more power than it already has.

No, she does not suit her name, she contemplates, as she rocks back and forward on the rocking chair. The knowledge that such a grotesque object occupies her head is bad enough; the thought of looking in the mirror and seeing it reflected through a transparent, crystal head is abhorrent to her.

'Come inside now, dear,' says the matronly nurse, guiding her by the elbow, 'It's time for dinner.' Crystal allows herself to be lead, like a lamb to the slaughter.

'You're a lucky girl tonight,' she says, seating Crystal comfortably at one of the tables, 'It's brains on toast for dinner.'

Crystal's eyes roll backwards, as something in her head explodes.

Balls of Steel

Karen Tay

Mrs Jiang was a 'Chinese immigrant' who lived three doors down from us. My father was a self-proclaimed racist.

'That Chinese immigrant.' He'd mutter to me, while stuffing his mouth full of crispy turkey bacon.

'Them Chinese immigrants – they take all the jobs that decent blokes like me could've had.'

The truth was, I liked Mrs Jiang. She'd play Chinese operas all the time on her cheap boom box. The voices were always unnaturally soprano, but the language! The language had lilts and curves that I couldn't follow. I would sit on her back porch for hours, listening to that wonderful opera warble until Dad called me back home.

I once asked her, 'Mrs Jiang, is there a Mr Jiang?'

She paused meaningfully, and I thought that maybe I had crossed a line.

'Ai-ya, Sally. You sound like a kid. Always asking this that.'

'Well, is there? Or was there?'

I was curious. I had never really looked at Mrs Jiang as a woman before. She had always been Mrs Jiang, or 'that Chinese immigrant'. It was as if I was looking at her for the first time. I noticed that her lips were shaped like a sweet, pink ribbon, and that her eyes were a beautiful, liquid brown. The scent of fried food hung heavily in the kitchen. I was captivated.

'Ai-ya. I tell you then story.'

'A story?'

I'd never heard a Chinese story before, and knowing Mrs Jiang, it could very well be a fairytale presented in her garbled version of

English. She saw me as even more of a child than my parents, even though I was sixteen at the time.

'About my man. Oh, such a handsome man, like what you call … Prince?'

'Yeah. Oh no, Mrs Jiang! I'm too old for Cinderella.

'What Cinderella?'

But her eyes were twinkling and merry. 'No, this better. Now listen! Mr Jiang, he come in to return book to friend. I was waiting for ride, and our eyes meet … and oh, how handsome he was … like prince. He look at me and it was like my … ahh, what do call in English? The thing that humans have after die?'

'Soul?'

'It was like my soul was singing beautiful music that only two of us could hear. And I lost my heart.'

'That's so lovely, Mrs Jiang. Truly.'

'Of course, Mr Jiang had balls of steel too.'

I almost choked on the cup of tea that she had given me. 'What?'

'Mr Jiang. He had balls of steel. That how he die. He crazy, tink he can fly plane high not crash. He fly so high. I look up, and my belly full of kid … then plane was coming down. I lost kid and husband in one day.'

I was in shock. I stared at Mrs Jiang, but she went on peeling onion. After a while, she looked up at me and shook her head, and I thought I saw a tear glisten out of the corner of her eye.

'Man with balls of steel, he bring nothing but heartache.'

More Turtles

Ross Lay

Howard never understood what a metre was until he measured his four-year-old son one day and discovered it was Kevin's exact height.

During his own childhood they'd had feet and inches. Yards and miles. At the TAB there was talk of furlongs. He'd even *heard* of leagues, and how twenty thousand was a long way under the sea.

But by the end of the primers there were centimetres. And millimetres, which were so small you could fit hundreds on a ruler. No-one's ruler, though, went up to a metre. Metres weren't invented until 1973, when a Sioux warrior measured 1.76 of them. Howard assumed that was a lot, Sioux warriors being so tough and all.

He'd not seen the last of the old measurements though. Miles, in particular, had real staying power.

Even during the year of the Sioux warrior, Howard's school still dished out 'Fifty Mile Club' badges for proud mothers to sew onto the uniforms of their athletic offspring. To be eligible you had to run fifty miles in six weeks, with teacher verification. No-one was surprised when Nathan Rua had his badge within a fortnight. But suspicions were aroused when all of room seven – even the girls – arrived at school one morning with Fifty Mile Club emblems newly-affixed to their thin chests.

Rumour had it they'd been running 'metric miles'. Howard hadn't heard of such things, but logic suggested they must be smaller than the kind he knew. When Miss Mason refused to adopt the new measurement, Howard withdrew his efforts in a protest that, sadly, went almost unnoticed.

He later worked out the 'metric miles' had been kilometres. No-one could agree how to pronounce 'kilometres'. In fact, the whole system seemed so difficult to master that Howard never seriously tried. Until the morning Kevin insisted on updating the ragged ladder that charted his progress up a wardrobe door.

Suddenly, everything metric became clear to Howard. His kitchen table was just under a metre high and perhaps two metres long. The knife that lay on it was a quarter Kevin's height, or – he checked the tape measure – twenty-five centimetres. 250 millimetres! He laughed aloud and thought of Vera Mason. Go on, test me now!

The return trip to the house where Howard deposited his slightly-confused son was seventy metres. He needed just 79,030 more, according to the conversion table in his diary, to make the Fifty Mile Club. He would do the distance today, then call in to inform Vera herself. She still lived, alone, in the town.

A road sign on the corner reminded Howard that his ex-wife lived 1.5 kilometres away, up the mountain that rose behind his home. It was not nearly enough. Gazing at the almost-perfectly-conical peak, Howard imagined fifteen hundred clones of his son, standing one upon another like King Yertle's victims in a chain that disappeared up into the clouds. 'More!' he shouted into the wind as he began running. 'More turtles!'

It Has No Name

Dena Thorne-Pezet

He looks older than I remember, perhaps heavier, a little grey. I watch him weave his way across the station; he's some distance away, yet so familiar he feels as close as my skin. Despite the crowds, I consume his every move; the set of his shoulders, the line of his jaw, the way his hair meets his collar at the nape of his neck, craving my touch. As he leaves my line of vision, I draw closer, feeding on nothing but the scent of him, before I buckle silently when he runs to greet his wife. It steals my breath, so that when he turns and holds me in his gaze, I am gasping and unsteady, the draw and spill of time ebbing at my feet.

Finally, he comes to me, his name repeated and unheard, his wife alert, negotiating the potential damage. Her face is sick with comprehension as she senses a taste still bitter; recalls seeing me in his eyes and catching me in his timbre, and relives the habit of a long remembered past. She understands who I am, although we never met.

We are speechless, still, without greeting or smile. Eventually he takes my hand cautiously in his, his back to his wife. With his eyes on mine he silently removes my glove, easing each finger from its warm smooth bed. Gently, he takes my palm to the plane of his cheek and simply holds my naked hand to his cold face, his warm lips, and with his eyes closed he breathes into my wrist, inhaling deeply, as water collects at his lashes. I scour his face, my bones raw, my breath close to his, when suddenly he pulls away and leaves, neither of us having spoken a word.

We were never lovers. There were no promises, whispers, lies or deceit. No words that named or anchored the want. But my dreams were laden with him, his face, his voice, his skin, his smell. The way he held my gaze when I spoke his name, the way my heart arrested when he spoke mine. My days were full of him, my nights saturated with his imagined presence. I dressed for him, laughed with him, spoke his name slowly, spoke it softly, catching my breath and rolling it sweetly over my tongue. But never once did his skin ever lie across mine.

I watch them go. He looks back at me, just briefly, just once. And I smile weakly, finally, in recognition. Bereft, I fumble in my bag for my ticket, understanding that time has moved on without me. I see it striking out alone across the station, as silent and unforgiving as a disappointed parent, shoulders hunched, sulking and harsh. And I stand bewildered, hopeful bags still packed and ready at my feet, meaning to keep up, but vainly watching it leave without me. With arms outstretched, palms to the sky, I call unanswered into its shadow, lonely as an abandoned old shoe lying in the dusty road.

Eleven-Eight Time

Suzanne Gee

Serena met Theo at Sunday brunch. She was entranced by the jazz, his fingers – so fast over the frets. On Monday, she invited him over. A thirties display designer, she owned her apartment, aspired to 'be creative'. She boiled rice, heated peanut oil, fried a whole snapper with pungent fresh ginger, then attacked the head with such relish he had to sit back and watch.

'This is the best bit,' she grinned. Her mischievous chopsticks trawled succulent flesh through soy sauce.

On Wednesday, he considered spending five dollars, inviting her for lamb chops, but worked out a lovely bass line at Pete's instead. On Thursday, they watched the Titanic go down on the big screen. She saw him cry, thought him sweet. At twenty-seven, with possessions that barely filled a station wagon, Theo earned money cleaning, but his real passion was recording a CD of original music with Pete.

Friday, Theo caught himself thinking of her long black hair, dancing eyes, and said to Pete;

'I could be getting into trouble here, mate.'

'I keep going over everything he says,' Serena admonished herself to a friend. 'He's so devoted to his music. I'd never even heard of eleven-eight time. I'm thinking so much more about my painting. Those beautiful hands …'

On Saturday they danced flamboyantly, then close. Her five-foot frame was at a perfect height, standing on the bottom stair, for her to fondle his hair, open his shirt. At the top of the stairs, his mouth and beautiful hands were on her nipples. On Sunday, his trousers hung in her closet; his guitar conversed with her easel, pasta bubbled over as they kissed.

A year later, on Monday, Theo says she's a fool for paying the water bill on time.

'Let them wait. Those bastards are making millions.' She grimaces, thinking of his friend Walter, waiting patiently for money to be repaid. On Tuesday, Theo's at rehearsal. Serena's glad he's gone. On Wednesday, Theo bleeds the brakes of her old Datsun for the WOF. 'The CV joints are going,' he says, 'but I'll sneak her through at twenty past five.' It passes. She jumps up and down, remembers she loves him.

On Thursday, picturing chicken and coconut, Serena says she'll make a curry.

'I'm going out,' he says. 'And Friday. A gig.' She frowns. He scolds, 'Do your art.' He stands outside in rancid boots, smokes a joint, drinks beer. Saturday, he sleeps.

Sunday it's gorgeous. Theo, foul in the mornings, drops his ashtray and the butts. Swears. Nervously, Serena asks if he'd like to go to the beach.

'Nah babe, I'm recording keyboards. Can I borrow the Datsun?'

'Keep it!' she spits. 'I'll help you load up!'

Theo considers this, then takes her hand, kisses her nose, her cheek. He chides.

'Don't be conventional, my love.'

Serena fumes at him, at the sunshine. She sees her easel unattended and sighs loudly, slams the studio door behind her. She pictures yellow ochre, a floating composition …

Morning, Noon and Night

Rowan Miller

Do you remember the time, that first time you took me to the bach? We got up before dawn and in the purple dark you took my hand and made me run down the cliff path, crashing down through gorse, the gorse catching in my hair, snatching at my face, my hands too fearful to hold on and, anyway, taken by your grip and pulled along and on and down the zigzag track to the beach?

How I screamed and laughed and said, 'Stop, I can't see a thing.' And you said, 'Trust me.'

You were showing off. You knew that track backwards and forwards, a path from the house to the water that spanned the thirty summers of your lifetime, gave you a history, made you bold with me.

You pulled the dinghy out from under the scrub, turned it over and skidded it into the estuary. You lifted me from dry sand to dry boat to save my city feet from the wet and with sure hands stroked us silently out into the deep.

And while we watched and waited for the sun I fell in love with you. I fell for your sleek rowing style. I fell like the rivulets of water, dashed with phosphorescence, falling from the oars. I fell and the sun rose and in that weighing of the scales our future was measured by a new light.

That golden hopeful future. Two dreamers, hell-bent on working the ends against the middle, kissing the sun – all that stuff. They seemed to have no endings or beginnings, those days. We were always in the middle of something. Some grand scheme that scorched our backs with possibility. We pushed and pulled at time, stretched its linear capacity to cram more into each day. We worked hard, cheated madly, ran fast. And then the babies came along. The carpet ankle-deep with toys and clutter. The books unread beside the bed. The days divided into eating and sleeping. Suddenly the grand scheme became yours and the chores were mine. And while you grew more confident, I felt confined and grew angry. I learned to turn my back on the day, close my eyes to the sun, sleep but not dream.

In the blaze of my anger I forgot several things. I forgot how you held each new-born child to the light and blessed our union for its best prize. I forgot how lonely it was for you to hold the dream alight while I slept. I forgot how well you rowed a boat.

I do a lot of counting. I count the reasons why you left, I count the years I stayed. As if somewhere in those numbers lies a mathematical equation that makes perfect sense. But I'm no good with maths. Regret only adds up to despair. I prod the embers and watch the day go down to ash, and count in ones; one egg, one spoon, a narrow bed, a single room.

War Games

Janet Tyler

One lunch, because Mark Roberts was home with the flu, Ben Alafi was allowed to join in the boys' tense game of war. He was on the side of The Commanders, the arch rivals of The Militants. I knew this because the boys used to force this information upon us during the reading class before lunch hour. Occasionally the names of the teams would change to The Invincibles, The Warlords, The Avengers, The Rebels, but the leaders were always the same. Stephen Maloney and Marcus Heal. Stephen and Marcus were the biggest boys in the year. They even claimed to have started shaving.

They knew about sex and the story went that Marcus had already done the pelvic thrust with a college girl three years his senior. Stephen and Marcus were best friends, although they fought on opposing sides. They were never killed though. That was part of their rules.

This day, however, when Ben Alafi was fighting for The Commanders, nobody, I think, can have clearly explained to him the rules. As usual, we were sitting on the grass eating our sandwiches, and starting rumours about various classmates and teachers. Out of the corner of my eye, I watched the progress of the war. At this point, collateral damage appeared at a minimum. There were no smashed windows or stubbed toes. I noticed stocky Ben hiding behind the fence leading to the lower field, biding his time, waiting for the right moment to pounce on the enemy. As Melissa was confirming the rumour that she had indeed French kissed Pete Dunaway at his house the previous weekend, one of the boys was shot down at the hands of Marcus. There was the usual ritual of death and celebration. The game continued.

Melissa was just about to continue with details of the whole tonguing process, when we were all distracted by the sudden movement. Ben had leapt from his hiding place. With the invisible automatic rifle cradled in his crooked arms, he shot at Marcus. But not only, as per the rules, was Marcus unassailable, he was the leader of The Commanders, the team Ben was supposed to be fighting for. Was this then a single-handed attempt at a coup? Was Ben attempting to level the playing field? Ben was a robust boy, but without a great following. He had gone out on a limb.

We watched in open-mouthed wonder, each, however, silently wishing the impossible – that Marcus would go down. 'Die, man, die!' Ben was shouting. Only of course Marcus kept standing there, looking at Ben as though he were the most idiotic thing in the world. 'But I am immortal,' Marcus said.

The results of Ben's blatant breach of the rules were multifold. There was real blood. There were 'accidentally' broken bones. Ben was first sent to hospital and then to Coventry by the war boys for the rest of term. He was never again allowed to join in their games. The Marcus and Stephen regime continued. The warning siren had been sounded.

Snow

Heather Snow

That was the winter that it snowed for five weeks straight. Heaviest
fall in nineteen years, people said. Late, too. Should be spring by now.
The newspapers charted it, from the early inches up into feet. Every
day was predicted to be the last. But it just kept coming down – some
days soft and peaceful, other days heavy and angry, pelting pedestrians
in the face and battling for life against tired windshield wipers. 'Cabin
fever' was on the tip of people's tongues; everybody had it, they said,
someone was bound to do something crazy.

Someone did. Wrote his lover's name in blood in the snow. It was
his blood. They didn't need to run the tests to determine that. He
never had the chance to get at hers. Crazy, they said. Used his own
blood. How 'bout that. Should have gone south, they said, gotten out,
not like he didn't have the money.

But he didn't go anywhere – just sat in that little rented room,
looking out at all the snow, till he started thinking mad thoughts. Sat
there thinking his mad, lonely thoughts right up till it stopped
snowing. That's when he got up out of his chair and made a trip
across town to Blue Baby Lou's.

That was the night the snow finally stopped. The sky had sealed up
its bountiful pouch and the heavy snow clouds gave one last drowsy
yawn and moved on. And the night was still. It had snowed all day,
and when the last dusting had been laid at dusk, nothing dared move.
The air hung and draped, waiting for a wind that never came. No one
was sure whether to believe it, so ominous and still that night air was.

But by eight o'clock the streets downtown had filled as restless
bodies rushed out into the new clear empty night. Doors of bars and

clubs were flung wide open and strong brassy notes of music billowed out from the jazz joints all up and down Garby Street. In the space around each doorway the music screamed out, enveloping, then twisting, reaching, dropping down, down into muted chaos as it continued to drift away from its doorway, overlapped by the next.

It was close to eleven o'clock when Victor Alexander buttoned his coat and put on his hat. Didn't know where he was going. Not really. Didn't matter. Just needed to go … somewhere; out. He hadn't been out of that room since the day he went to visit her with the little bracelet wrapped around his fingers, buried deep in his pocket. That was just before the snow, and when that started up, he just didn't bother going out *again*. (Moira, Moira, where are you?) He stuffed his hand in his coat pocket to find the bracelet that was no longer there. Was no longer anywhere. On a street somewhere, perhaps, beneath all the snow.

Come Home Chrome Dome

Lesley Wallis

'I'll traverse the key issues on the whiteboard in a mind-mappy sort of way,' she said.

We sat. We breathed. The sun glittered timidly on the winter windows. We poured glasses of water from the tall jugs on the tables. I noted idly that the peppermints in the small glass dishes sat untouched. Did everyone suspect sabotage or were they merely protecting their ageing and increasingly fragile teeth? I crossed and recrossed my legs. There isn't really much you can do when it comes to making a mind-mappy sort of thing into something new. Things like that have a habit of staying the same.

My new lover is bald. I am having to learn new things with him, not the least being the thrill of making love with a shiny-headed man. There are no passionate hands caressing tangled curls or snaking tendrils on muscled necks – but they are seventies thrills, as old-hat as Flower Power. Nowadays we all enjoy much sharper, smoother pleasures in our streamlined lives. My bald, bold lover is fantastically athletic for his age.

The whiteboard told corporate lies in coherent frameworks and policy paradigms in a trail of non-permanent red and blue marker pens. They cluttered the board like bloodstains and flowering, spreading bruises.

'It is imperative that we identify our policy expectations and what partnership *really* means,' she said.

I know what partnership really means. I met him on a train. I saw him first. I sat down beside him but I did not speak.

I never catch trains. I am a woman who likes to control where she is going. I am a driver, not a rider. This time, I caught a train. This time, he did too.

'We need to ensure that we consistently engage in meaningful dialogue,' she said as she stepped forward and pulled the top off a blue felt marker. Her black suit was expensive but that hadn't stopped it puckering and creasing as it stretched over the soft, swollen expanse of her thighs. She wrote 'M D' in large letters on the whiteboard. The row in front of me slumped, heads dipped; new doodles started making their flowery way up margins.

I know what meaningful dialogue means. The train was late. It stopped in one of the seven tunnels that it must pass through on the twenty-minute journey into the city. We sat beside each other, breathing in the dark for ten minutes. The air between us crackled and bucked. We got off the train together.

These days, whiteboards, strategic plans, paradigms and frameworks do not interest me much. He is fantastically athletic for his age.

The Carp

Richard von Sturmer

Gazing at the scales of an orange and grey carp as it passes by in the aquarium, what first appears to be a covering of metallic plates now becomes an intricate arrangement of small, overlapping fans. The curved edge of each fan is decorated by a series of minute feathers so that the whole carp, losing its conventional armature, is transformed into a creature of the air.

Rising effortlessly to the top of its sky-blue tank, the carp then glides down to the sand at the bottom. Its round, elastic mouth blows into the grains of sand and tiny pebbles, just as a Japanese maiden, dressed in her summer kimono, would kneel down and blow gently onto the surface of a pond.

My reverie is disrupted when I walk outside. The autumn leaves are being scattered in the air, creating orange flashes against the background of a grey sky. As I zip up my jacket, a fin disappears behind a low-lying shrub, and a liquid eye, left hovering in mid-air, fades into the eye of a sea-lion who sits on a concrete slab and stares morosely into space. The zoo itself seems in a state of suspension, the sudden cold of the past few days having kept away the usual crowd of visitors. I start walking up the hill towards the lion cages and exit beyond, when I notice that a child, little more than a year old, has been left by itself in a pushchair. With a sudden movement, the child pulls off a bright blue mitten and throws it on the ground.

Back at home, I read in my book of Chinese symbols that the carp is an emblem of perseverance because it struggles against the current, and that it has the potential, leaping up the white back of a waterfall, to become a great and benevolent dragon. I try to picture such a dragon, but all that comes to mind is the image of five small fingers spread out like a fan.

Growth

Louise Wrightson

It happened quickly. One morning, Fair called from her bedroom. She showed me a fern growing in her wardrobe.

'It wasn't here yesterday, mum,' she said. She reached underneath it and pulled out her gumboots.

I waved her goodbye on the school bus and went into the house. There was a vine twisted around a coat hanger, too.

It was very humid. When Fair came home, we lay on the couch with ice-cubes on our foreheads.

'Bloody weather,' Tom muttered. 'It's gone completely haywire.'

He clicked a light switch up and down. Nothing happened. A supplejack had poked an exploratory finger in through a window. It had pulled the light fitting from the wall.

The storm started with an explosion of thunder. The gutters couldn't hold the rain. Water covered the outside of the windows like sheets of silk. The wind came from all directions. It uprooted bushes and tossed the birds around.

When the weather settled, an orange sun appeared. Steam rose from the ground and drifted through the house.

I threw out rotting vegetables and scrubbed at patches of lichen on the walls. I found weird looking fungi multiplying under the couch. Seedlings had pushed up between the floorboards in the laundry.

Outside, the trees closed in on the house. Branches tapped at the windows.

Tom headed into town for help. He came back to tell us that the road was blocked by slips and the power lines were down. We were trapped.

We moved up to the attic when the growth inside the house reached the window-sills.

We heated tinned food on the primus. The water in the header tank tasted slimy. Tom painted 'S O S' on the roof.

'What's that mean?' asked Fair.

'Send our saviour,' replied Tom wryly. He sharpened the machete.

We told Fair it was a test of our survival skills. If we passed, we would be rescued by helicopter.

We moved again when the top of a tree forced the trap door in the attic open.

There was a burnt clearing on a hill behind the house. We hacked a path to it through the thick undergrowth.

'It's safe here,' Tom reassured me. 'The ground is sterile. Nothing can grow.' He strung up a tarpaulin and set traps for birds.

On Fair's sixth birthday, we wove her a flax kete and filled it with berries. I thought about birthday cakes. I looked down at where our house had been. Only the chimney was still visible, like a white candle in green icing.

I was dreaming of soap when Tom shook me awake. Fair was asleep. Leaves were tangled in her hair. Tom pointed a finger at the faint down on her cheek.

'It's moss,' he said hoarsely.

His fingernail was a black crescent. A shoot sprouted from it. The stem ran under the nail like a silver stream. The root branched out to meet the rising moon.

The Gardenia Tree

Kellyana Morey

The sun doesn't set until 8.46pm in January. It hangs on, until one longs for it to travel to the other end of the world. The houses squat, pastel-faded and sunburnt, resolutely square. The lawns are always bare, tidy. It was like nobody ever quite imagined that they would be around long enough to plant a tree and watch it grow. People are sitting outside, fanning themselves on front porches and on the back stairs. They drink lemonade and beer, passing the sweating glasses and cans over their foreheads, as they do in the movies. Blowflies die slowly in the dull heat.

Ruth sighs, then shivers.

The city breathes again as the coolness of evening meanders past brick and tile and street lamps to settle on skin. A breeze floats across the darkness. It smells like rain.

'The key won't work. I'm locked out.' She holds the key out to him. He looks out the window, fingers steepled under his chin. Slivers of scalp shine through his thick hair.

A gardenia grows at the gates of his house. The roots have ruptured the concrete footpath. It has flowers, waxy blooms that are slightly bruised around the edges, the hearts still perfect. The blooms are carried inside, cradled in the palm of his hand.

Shelves in the kitchen hold a collection of Japanese bowls, cups and chopstick holders. 'People give me these things.' He shrugs, not understanding it. He considers for a moment, then smiles at her before selecting two white cylinders. Tea is poured. The porcelain is so thin that Ruth can see the shadow of her fingertips when she lifts the cup to drink. A blessing trapped between layers of clay and gauze.

And he talks. He came here forty-seven years ago to search for something better, better than the pictures he carries on the back of his brown eyes. His words melt into each other, indigo and voodoo. The radio is switched on, opera first, then community programming. The sound of Samoan women singing church songs settles over her. The hours swim past, some noticed, others neglected. Outside, the rain hisses and she is tired, tired, tired.

Two woven mats lie on the floor, a tivaevae at each end. Between the mats, three gardenias float in a bowl. 'To encourage beautiful dreams,' he explains. 'Te moemoea, the dream.' He kisses Ruth once, twice, and whispers, 'Sleep.'

The rain grows heavier and the sound of his breathing deepens into sleep.

She thinks of his hands, the way they moved in delicious rhythm with his voice when he spoke. They are hands that write poetry in the air, between the silences. The city traffic sounds like the ocean at night crashing on the shores of a place that none of us calls home.

Magic

Pip Robertson

They passed the stage and a gathering crowd in the morning. 'Later,' her mother had said. 'Now is no time to dawdle.'

The mother shopped as if following a strategic map, accumulating bags and packages at each counter. Bewildered, the girl hurried to keep up, wondering at her mother's immunity to glints and gleams. Unlike the girl she was never lured by shop displays. Purchases were made with a firm 'because.' An eggbeater because the old one had rusted. A winter coat because that green one was too small.

At midday they sat in a booth in the tearooms at the bottom of the building and ate dainty tiered sandwiches. The mother talked about being a girl, seeing the same magician in the same store, how elderly he seemed even then. Free from instruction or reprimand, that conversation was a luxury. The mother wasn't one for idle chatter.

They went back for the afternoon performance. The magician, smart in his top hat, suit and shiny shoes, shuffled across the stage. He explained that he was very old, making the children yell three hellos, louder and louder until he could hear. For his first act he needed a volunteer. Arms sprouted and the girl thrust hers up among them. Pointing dramatically, he picked the girl in green, lingering on the 'r' like a drum-roll. Other children, cross-legged and envious, shifted to look as she walked between them onto the stage. Up close, the magician smelled like old clothes and peppermint. It sounded as if he had a cold, breath rattling in and out. He showed her how she was to hold a scarf, making a cup with his palm, but his hand shook. He talked in ragged bursts. She couldn't understand.

'Take it,' he gasped, 'take it,' shoving the red silk at her, his face darkening. The crowd murmured, puzzled by the performance. The magician gave an awkward sideways bow. He reached for his other arm then, balance lost, toppled to lie near the girl's feet. His hat rolled a small way, then stopped.

Hushed.

Still.

The girl stood on stage, suddenly alone. The audience sat expectant, then hesitant, then adults flurried forward, shrouding the old man, bustling her back to where she couldn't see.

After her mother dies, she sorts out the house and finds the scarf. Kept all this time.

She had discovered it in her hand when they left the store. She had wanted to return it to the magician, but her mother took it like an unclean thing, tucking it quickly into one of their shopping bags. It is improbable that it rained every time they went to town, implausible. But that is how she pictures it, the streets wet and grey, her mother just ahead with umbrella and handbag, striding determinedly forward. She thinks about this and her mother's monitored hospital death, and about the old magician's heart, which stopped beating so publicly and suddenly. From living to lifeless.

A final and unscheduled act of magic.

Crown Lynn

Cherie Barford

The Afro-comb, its grey teeth evenly spaced and plastic, reminded the young woman of old hammerhead sharks, their grisly throats pincushions of stingray spines. She coiled her black frizzy hair into a bun. Secured it with a clip. 'My name is So'ogalafo,' she said to the mirror. 'Bleeced to meet you.'

So'ogalafo smoothed her dress, checked that she'd put a clean apron in her handbag and that yesterday's taro and fish weren't clinging to her teeth. Then, hips swaying, she stepped into Wingate Street and the lukewarm morning that counted for summer in New Zealand.

'Get work at Crown Lynn or Cambridge Clothing,' her uncle had told her before she left Samoa. 'Be a good girl. Work hard at your job. Send money home. Go to church.'

She got a job at Crown Lynn Potteries because she ached for the feel of the humid earth of her village. It was too cold to walk in her aunty's garden without shoes.

So'ogalafo was shocked by the heaviness of her first handful of clay, by the way it stank and stuck to her fingers and her nose when she itched it. The other women at her lunch table laughed. They had names like Betty, Tui, Marge and Rangi. They renamed her Crown Lynn because it was easy to say and that's where they all worked.

When So'ogalafo arrived at work her boss looked worried. He was picking up cups, pulling at their handles.

'There's been complaints,' Tui whispered. 'Handles are falling off cups in public places. People were scalded on the train this morning.'

The women became anxious. What if the place closed down? They were used to it. To each other. So'ogalafo crossed her fingers. Would her family recall her? Would she have Christmas at home?

'Not bloody likely,' said Rangi. 'You're too valuable over here. All that money you're sending back. Why don't you hang on to a bit? Treat yourself to a movie or a lipstick.'

So'ogalafo shook her head. She was still shaking it when her boss pulled her over to stand beside a car, a Vauxhall, parked on a bed of cups. On its roof was a tray set for morning tea with Crown Lynn pottery.

'What strong cups!' exclaimed the photographer. 'Smile honey.'

So'ogalafo did as she was told. Everyone cheered. Her smile widened.

When the newspaper printed the photograph, So'ogalafo cut it out and sent it to her family. The caption read, 'Miss Crown Lynn handles spilt milk.'

Her uncle, a priest, wrote back. Her cousin, a New Zealand citizen, translated the message for So'ogalafo's workmates:

> *Dear Crown Lynn*
>
> *Thank you for the money for repairs to our church. Your Kiwi name suits you. You are already famous. Be good and remember your beloved family and congregation.*
>
> *God bless*
> *Uncle Sione*

That night So'ogalafo looked at herself in the mirror. Smiled. 'Bleeced to meet you. My name is Crown Lynn.'

Jonah at Kapiti

Bill Direen

The beach is a litter of branches, trunks and twigs. Waves are unflapping contentedly enough now, but logs are lying near the tide-line where they were pitched effortlessly by a recent storm. A gull is lying breast upwards, plumage drying in mats.

A man is standing at the foot of dunes staring over a slope of driftwood, washed, sanded and baked brittle, over steaming trunks, the seaswell that resembles the curved backs of whales, over it all to a long, dark island. The spine of the island is like that of a tuatara. It climbs from the south to the crest in six stages then drops quickly at the head. The sun hangs above the northern end. Some twigs crack with the heat. High above, cloud is forming. The air is salty and pongy with decaying matter.

The boy stops to collect stones and shells from among the gravel, a red handkerchief is hanging from his pocket.

Now the man is waving at the boy and calling. The sea expands. The boy doesn't hear him. He is positioning some stones along the ridge of a split log. The sea is deepest green, repealing even the dense bush of the island whose shelves mark discrete ecological communities on this the leeward, the visible side. Rata are flaming, filled with honey-seeking birds, and the island seems not only to live but to speak.

The words are barely recoverable, but the boy hears them and is not surprised. He picks up a handful of stones and throws them in the air. He watches as an official boat carries registered visitors into the shadow of the island to observe the birdlife and the flora. The passengers intend to climb to the top. They want to look out towards Australia. Some wonder how the island will look on the other side.

Is it a mirror reflection of the mainland flank? Or will the peaks level out to a wide, salt-swept plain? And the sea, will there be more islands freckling the water all the way to the horizon? How can they know that at the top the island stops? There is no other side. On the windward side it plummets down sheer cliff to a slim ledge of golden stone just wide enough for a man and a boy to walk along.

A whale is in the water, swimming the long scoop of the channel, between mainland and island. The scientists and tourists on the island gasp as one. Why does the man look so concerned? That's it, the boy is no longer there. The man searches along the shore. He scoures the dunes. Now he has stripped off and dived into the whale-concealing foam, but he will not find the boy out there either. He will not find him today, nor tomorrow, nor the day after that.

China Doll

Andrew M Bell

Rain. Some cultures believe that when it rains the sky god is weeping. The sky god has not tears enough for Chulia Street.

Monsoonal rain. Rad and Brett sipped Chinese tea and studied the forlorn-looking beach through the curtain of water falling in runnels from the bamboo roof of the café.

Brett ate a spring roll with audible pleasure. 'Kids, eh? Look at those little buggers having the time of their lives.'

Unperturbed by the rain, two small Malay boys were taking turns to drag each other along the beach in an old tyre. Periodically, they collapsed on the sand, weakened by exertion and irrepressible mirth.

The boys' exuberance touched off a restlessness in Brett. 'It feels like a long time since I got laid.'

'Chulia Street?'

They ate Hainan chicken rice in Chulia Street and waited for the inevitable. An old man with a dark, weather-beaten face approached. 'You want girls?'

Rad wondered if dens of iniquity all employed the same interior designer. The low lighting, the cosy rattan nooks and the whisper of chrome in the semi-darkness all combined to produce a veneer of respectability designed to deflect any official scrutiny.

They bought their snaggle-toothed guide a large bottle of Anchor beer and he melted into the background.

Two girls were brought over, one Indian and one Chinese. They were both attractive, but they were light and shade in personality. The Indian girl was bubbly, laughing and displayed a good command of English. The Chinese girl was subdued and unsmiling. Rad put it down to culturally bred shyness and a poor command of English.

Brett swiftly staked his claim to the Indian girl, 'Thirty-five ringgit, one hour,' the bar owner said.

The Chinese girl flicked off the lights and slipped out of her black cocktail dress. As though performing a ritual, she arranged each item of clothing over the back of a chair and then lay on the bed like an offering.

Enough light trickled into the room for Rad to admire her small, perfect body. She projected an air of fragility like a porcelain figurine.

When Rad tried to kiss her, she turned her face away. Her hand went straight to his cock. When she deemed it ready, she lubricated herself with KY jelly. Rad felt as though he had been plugged in.

When it was over, she went straight to the ensuite to douche. It was as if his sperm was a virulent invader that she must purge without delay.

As she made up for her next customer, she gazed wistfully into the mirror as though it was a portal through which she might escape to the kampong, where her brothers played on the beach like those boys Rad had seen that afternoon.

Back on Chulia Street the rain kept falling, engorging the drains until they were heady with decay.

A Matter of Taste

Claire Beynon

It is no secret. I cannot resist them. Sour worms and body parts. I have a passion for Pascall's that is difficult to disguise. There have been times when I have had to beg my family to hide them from me. I have even been known to hide them from myself. At the very least, I keep them stashed away on the highest shelf in our kitchen, sealed in a lime and rose floral tin.

I cannot help feeling a little foolish about this. After all, I am no youngster, and should be beyond such sweet seductions. I control myself reasonably well most of the time, but this morning – after an extended and particularly well-managed dry period – I was tipped into craving these delights again.

It was just before nine when I arrived outside the white stone building. The gallery door was ajar, but the place was quiet. There was no one in the front room. Large paintings flanked the walls like sentries. I caught myself saluting as I walked past them, heading straight for the concealed door in the back wall of the gallery. I had phoned the day before to let the staff know I would be coming, but nevertheless I knocked before pushing the door open.

A hive of sound greeted me. The entire team was in the stockroom, intently unpacking a stack of large slatted crates and smaller oblong boxes. They beckoned me over to see what it was they were uncovering.

The containers were filled with body parts. Mine at home are soft and sugared. Noses (mostly) as well as teeth and lips, and the occasional slightly misshapen ear, all in various artificial shades of pastel. The bits in the crates, however, were dry and dusty, cast in gritty concrete and palest pink plaster – several hundred pieces layered loosely one on top of the other. Some appeared to have been chipped in transit, causing great consternation and provoking exclamations from even the most uncommunicative in the company. Evidently the artist had not packed the components of this installation meticulously enough in preparation for the journey south.

It took a while for me to notice that the uniformed courier was still in the room. The staff must have insisted he stay while they unpack the first few crates. Their excitement and delight forbade him from leaving. He stood a slight distance from the group, as nonchalant and unblinking as a lizard. No matter that today his name was down on the company list to deliver nine crates of body parts, and a heavy, glass-fronted cabinet to display them in.

I confess to thinking, 'That cupboard could do with a good rubbing-down with fine steel wool and a few coats of clear varnish. And that glass wants a thorough clean.'

Silver Bullet: The Dorm Version

Michael Laws

Her name is Joanna and she's sitting on top of the automatic washing machine with her skirt hitched up and her slim legs open. The spin cycle has just finished. And there's that *look* on her face – like melting chocolate.

I'd taken her out to the movies. Well, sort of. She'd borrowed her old lady's car, paid for the tickets and bought the half-time ice-creams. But, hey, I'm a hostel boy. We're made to mooch.

It was *The Exorcist* and I'd seen it the week before in Palmerston North. We were meant to be at some bursary-seminar thing – religion in puritan England, being held at the Girls' High. Bugger that, we all agreed as we were going down in the back of the mini-van. So we went to the morning session but, somehow, got lost between the Girls' High library and the Girls' High toilet block. Ended up at the Odeon in the Square. All except Pratt – a proper dick licker. Anyway, we line up in our school uniforms with parkas over the top of them so that no-one can tell that we're under 18. And we make Hardy buy the tickets because he's got the most convincing bum fluff.

The Exorcist. Jesus. It scares the total crap out of us. Even old 'Zulu' Taumata – I mean even *he* goes picket white. We all reckoned afterwards that it wasn't so much the plot or the puke or the lighting or anything like that. Nah, it was that fucking music. Put us right off our Jaffas.

Anyway, now we've got instant celebrity status because we've seen the movie and it's not due in Wanganui until next week. So we're thinking: Now if we were scared shitless, then what will this movie do to the chicks? And when they're all beside themselves, then they'll be easy. *Ea-sy*. Because we've seen it and know where all the scary bits are and we'll be um, y'know … *ready*.

Strange isn't it? The things that make perfect sense in a double accounting period and how they can seem so bloody stupid when you're sitting in a packed Embassy on a Friday night. Because it happens again: I go absolutely phobic. Although it's even worse the second time round. You get all the stuff you missed the first time. Mate, I'm fucking *pet-ri-fied*.

So we drive back to her parents' place, right? And I'm still shaking and seeing demons floating everywhere with the green eyes and the maggoty faces and the pus sores. And Joanna's asking me if *I'm* all right and do I usually sweat like this in the dead of winter? Turns out she thinks the whole movie was a bit lame. Like heads can do 360 degree turns and still keep talking, yeah right, and why didn't those stupid people just turn the lights on. All that sort of shit.

So I'm thinking this is one stone-cold, frigid bitch. I'm *never* going to shoot the silver bullet. And, like, we've been going out for bloody months. Haven't even had a decent feel of her tits.

Then she goes and sits on top of the Fisher and Paykel. And turns it on.

Finalists in Tandem Press's Short Short Story Competition

Burgeoning – Rhonda Bartle

The Butterfly Orchid – Virginia Fenton

Four Fish – James Norcliffe

Night Watchman – Judith White

Nor'wester – Tracey Edginton

Queen of the Night – Penelope Bieder

Silver Bullet: The Dorm Version – Michael Laws

Spain-ish Hearts – Katy Dugdale

Sunday at the Beach with George – Isa Moynihan

This Is How Good the Coffee Is – Denise Sammons

The Truckie – Maureen Langford

'True Facts About Girls Who Smoke and Drink Liquor' – Jane Bissell

notes on contributors

ALASTAIR AGNEW, born in Brazil, lived in Northern Ireland and Southern England before moving to New Zealand, aged seven. He grew up in Mataura and later lived in Gore, Dunedin, Melbourne, Britain and the Netherlands. He spent the nineties in Spain and recently moved to Sydney. Previous work has appeared in *Sport* and *Landfall*.

RAEWYN ALEXANDER's paternal ancestors arrived here on the *Lady Jocelyn* three generations ago. She was born in Hamilton, fleeing to Auckland and the wide world ASAP. Two children have somehow survived her terrible housekeeping. Writing novels, stories, poems and nonfiction leaves little time for vacuuming.

GEOFF ALLEN was born in Auckland in 1961 and lives in Tawa. Art school dropout. Met Fomison and Clairmont, 1981. Acted in the film *Merry Christmas, Mr Lawrence*. Started writing plays when unemployed. Wrote first publication, *He Lies Down*, at the Whitireia Polytechnic writing course. His wife is a Methodist minister. He has three sons.

JOHN ALLISON lives in Lyttelton, teaches in Christchurch and writes elsewhere. He has recently completed a book of stories, several of which have appeared in *Metro*, *Takahe*, and *The Third Century*. His poetry is widely published, and his most recent book, *Stone Moon Dark Water*, was published in 1999 by Sudden Valley Press.

CHERIE BARFORD was born in Auckland in 1960 to a German–Samoan mother and a Palagi father. She grew up in West Auckland where she lives and is working on, with the support of a Creative NZ grant, her third collection of poetry, *Westie File*. Her work has been anthologised in various publications.

RHONDA BARTLE lives to write in New Plymouth. In 1999 she won the BNZ Katherine Mansfield Short Story Award. Her first novel is due out soon. She's been saying since the age of ten that she'd write a book one day. She can finally shut up about it now.

ANDREW M. BELL was born in Rotorua in 1957 and has recently moved to Christchurch from Wellington with his wife, Christine, and son, Thomas. With 'Wellywood' flourishing, he is adapting his play, *The Reluctant Messiah*, for the screen. He has been published in England, Israel, Australia and New Zealand.

CLAIRE BEYNON was born in South Africa, but Dunedin has been home since 1994. A full-time artist and mother of three (children and cats), she writes poetry and short fiction and is fascinated by the powerful connections between words, images and the unconscious. Commended in recent *Takahe* and *SIWA* short story competitions, she was second runner-up 1999 *Sunday Star-Times* competition. Her work has been published locally, and by *Chicken Soup* in the US.

PENELOPE BIEDER, journalist, was born in Palmerston North in 1949, fifteen minutes after her twin sister. The second short story she has written is the first of her fiction published. Happiest in dreadful old clothes in her garden on the Coromandel, she has been known to run and hide when unexpected visitors arrive.

JANE BISSELL was born in Seattle Washington, USA in 1956, and now lives in Whangaparaoa north of Auckland in a little house overlooking the Hauraki Gulf. Late last year she left her career as a manager in the air express industry to begin writing full-time. This is her first published story and she is working on her first novel.

DOROTHY BLACK began her writing career with the *Otago Daily Times'* children's pages. After marriage she wrote successful plays for women's drama festivals. She has published *Tales for Pippa*, and won writing competitions in New Zealand, NSW and London. Dorothy was a reporter for local newspapers and *NZ Government* magazine. She published a mystery murder *The O'Connor Affair*. Retired, she lives in Auckland.

JANE BLAIKIE was born in New Plymouth in 1960. She moved to Wellington five years later and has been there more or less ever since. She trained as an accountant but it didn't add up. Nowadays she tutors part-time at Whitireia Polytechnic.

TAMZIN BLAIR is twenty-three and lives in Kaiwaka, Northland. She has had one children's book published, *The Best Treasure Ever*, and her second book, *Fiddle Middle Jiddle Sticks*, is on the way.

MICHAEL BLAND was born in Dunedin in 1962 and schooled in Tokoroa. A non-Qantas award-winning journalist, his work has been rejected by some of New Zealand's finest publications. Domiciled near Cambridge with one wife and two children, his interests include watching television and picking his nose – often simultaneously.

PETER BLAND lives in London where he is poetry reviewer for *The London Magazine*. He is working on a new collection of poems, *Borderlands*, due early in 2001 from Carcanet, who published his *Selected Poems* in 1998.

BERNARD BROWN has spent forty years as a law teacher urging barristers and solicitors to make short points in long drawn-out and expensive paragraphs. This story is his opportunity to do the opposite.

DIANE BROWN is a novelist and poet. Auckland-born and bred, she has recently moved to Dunedin. She is the author of *Before the Divorce we go to Disneyland*, a combination of prose and poetry, and the novel *If the Tongue Fits*, both published by Tandem Press.

DAVID LYNDON BROWN is a writer, poet, playwright and teacher in Auckland. He has been published in several anthologies here and abroad. He is a natural blond.

RACHEL BUCHANAN lives in Melbourne but is working on a series of connected stories about New Zealand. Her short stories have been published in *Landfall*, *Sport* and *Takahe*.

LINDA BURGESS, who believes that no one gives a toss when or where she was born, is the author of two-and-half novels, a short story collection and a travel book, *Allons Enfants*. In theory writing another novel, she spends the megabucks she makes from writing on her gorgeous new granddaughter Lucie.

RO CAMBRIDGE created 'Child's Play' by condensing an episode from a longer work and found it interesting to discover how few words could still contain the essence of the original. She has written very little in the last couple of years except in connection with her work in arts administration/marketing, but her strong childhood identification as a storywriter remains in spite of a lack of material evidence.

TRUDI CAMERON was born in 1966 and grew up in South Otago. She currently lives on the Hibiscus Coast, where she teaches English and journalism at Orewa College. She has also worked as a radio copywriter. 'Good for a Laugh' is her first published fiction.

JERRY CHUNN was born in Greymouth in 1923, educated at St Bede's College, Christchurch and Otago Medical School, and did a post-graduate medical degree at Edinburgh. An allergy specialist in Auckland until 1992, he is now retired. He has published two books: *Am I Allergic?* (1992) and *High Bouncing Lover* (1998), a miscellany of prose and poetry.

VICTORIA CLEAL, twenty-eight, grew up in Auckland and is now based in Sydney, where she is a subeditor. She has been published in Australia's *Overland* and *Ulitarra*.

DOUG COUTTS was born in 1955 and lives in Wellington. A freelance writer with diverse credits – *Shortland Street*, *McPhail & Gadsby* and the Master Plumbers' Association – he did Harry

Ricketts's creative writing workshop at Victoria University in 2000, suspecting there were other things to write for than groceries.

MARGARET CRAWFORD was born in 1946 in South Africa. She trained as a social worker and later worked in community development and adult education. On coming to New Zealand in 1995 she joined Phill Mann's Greenroom writing group, which still meets regularly. She lives in Island Bay, Wellington with a view of Cook Strait and believes she has found Godzone.

GRANT DALE was born in Dunedin in 1971 and grew up in nearby Mosgiel. Following school he gained a science degree, worked for three years in university administration, then revelled in a two-year overseas experience. He has recently completed Owen Marshall's fiction writing course at Aoraki Polytechnic in Timaru.

JACKIE DAVIS was born in New Plymouth in 1963 and now lives in Palmerston North. Her fiction has appeared in *Metro*, *The Third Century* and she has been placed in numerous short story and poetry competitions. She is the current recipient of the Lillian Ida Smith Award.

LISETTE DE JONG was born in 1969 and grew up in various parts of the North Island. Fear of a dull existence drove her to Auckland after she had finished school, overseas when she hit twenty-five, and producing a television show when the age of thirty loomed. She is an actor constantly between jobs. This is her first published story.

BILL DIREEN, after years of making music, poetry and theatre, now describes himself simply as a writer. He has always worked without undue regard for labels, cliques or marketing strategies. Suspicious of the underground and horrified by the overground, he lives in Waihenga.

KATY DUGDALE lives in Auckland, where she was born in 1963. She has spent twelve years of her adult life living in other countries. She has never been married, never been to Spain and knows no one called Brian.

TRACEY EDGINTON is a trained journalist working in Auckland. Born in 1971 in Timaru, she studied English at Otago, followed by a three-year stint overseas. Since returning in 1996, she has worked in public relations and freelance writing. This is the first time her fiction has been published.

DAVID EGGLETON is a hybrid: a part-Rotuman Islander born in central Auckland in 1952, he now resides in Dunedin's North End in a communal household. He travels around New Zealand frequently, and is also an intermittent visitor to Australia and the Pacific, looking at everything with a writer's eye.

KIYOHIRO EJIMA, 1954–1979 Tokyo, baby, boy, student, factory worker, fieldworker, shop assistant, bodyguard, traffic-counter, funpark-creator, screenprinter; 1979–1983 Queenstown, father, painter, kitchenhand; 1983–2000 Takaka, father, painter, sculptor, musician, builder, image-creator.

JAN FARR was born years ago on the West Coast, schooled in Christchurch, raised children in Auckland and found in later life that things really were better in Wellington.

FRANK FELL was born in London in 1955. His poems have been published in journals, chap-books and anthologies in Britain and New Zealand, including the *New Exeter Book of Riddles* (1999). He lives near Nelson where he teaches English at NMIT and works part-time as an agricultural labourer.

VIRGINIA FENTON was born in Auckland in 1974. She has had poetry published in *Sport*, *Mutes & Earthquakes*, *Poetry New Zealand*, *Printout* and *Takahe*, and fiction in *The Picnic Virgin*. Her plays have been performed at the 1996 and 1998 Wellington Fringe Festivals. She has lived in Wellington, London and Taipei.

VICTORIA FRAME lives in Herald Island, West Auckland, with her husband and son. She writes sporadically and erratically. This is her third short short story published in the series.

JANIS FREEGARD lives in Wellington with her cat, Spike, and many inflatable baby aliens. She was born in South Shields, England, in 1963, but has lived in New Zealand most of her life. She has had work published in *Takahe* and *Eat These Sweet Words*.

JEANETTE GALPIN was born in Wellington and lives in the Rangitikei. She is the author of five books of nonfiction and a variety of short stories; her writing has also been anthologised and broadcast. Her latest book is the biography *Bessie: portrait of a master* (Maungatiro Press, 2000).

SUZANNE GEE grew up in Manaia and captained the Hawera High School 1st XI hockey team in 1970. She lives in Ponsonby. She photographed 500 weddings and 1008 families as Sue Gee but reckons the time has come to begin her new life as author. She attended the Aoraki fiction-writing course in 1999.

LINDA GILL was born in London in 1937. She has an MA (Hons) in French from the University of Auckland and has been a teacher, mother, artist, travel writer and art critic. *Living High* won the 1984 Boardman Tasker Prize for Mountain Literature and *Letters of Frances Hodgkins*, which she edited, was short-listed for the Montana Book Award in 1994.

KATIE HENDERSON was born in 1961. In 1999, a short story escaped from her and won the novice section of the BNZ Katherine Mansfield Awards. She currently lives in Torbay on Auckland's North Shore with her husband and three children, and has various works awaiting release.

GEOFF HENSHAW was born in Auckland in 1965. He obtained a PhD in Chemistry from the University of Auckland and has worked as a scientist in England and New Zealand. He has co-authored numerous academic papers but this is his first published work of fiction.

DAVID HILL is a fulltime writer and part-time astronomer living in New Plymouth. His novels and plays for young adults and children are published in nine countries. He still gets lots of rejection slips, and he still can't afford to retire.

KEVIN IRELAND lives in Devonport, on Auckland's North Shore. His thirteenth book of poems, *Anzac Day*, was published in 1997. His fourth book of fiction, *The Craymore Affair*, appeared earlier this year. His memoir, *Under the Bridge & Over the Moon*, was published in 1998, and won the Montana prize for History and Biography.

TIM JONES divides his time between writing, being a husband and father, and maintaining websites. His poetry has appeared in various New Zealand journals, most recently *Southern Ocean Review* and *JAAM*, and his fiction in magazines and anthologies in the UK, the USA, Australia, Canada and New Zealand.

KAPKA KASSABOVA is an Auckland-based novelist and poet. Her first novel, *Reconnaissance*, won the Commonwealth Writers' Prize for best first book in the Southeast Asia and South Pacific region and was shortlisted for the NZ Montana Book Awards. Her second novel, *Love In The Land Of Midas*, is due late in 2000. She is currently co-writing the Globetrotter travel guide to Delhi, Jaipur and Agra.

PHIL KAWANA (Ngaruahinerangi, Ngati Ruanui, Ngati Kahungunu ki Wairarapa) is a writer and broadcaster who was born in Hawera in 1965. As well as appearing in several anthologies, he has also published two books, *Dead Jazz Guys* (1996) and *Attack of the Skunk People* (1999). His first novel is already overdue.

SHERIDAN KEITH was born in Wellington in 1942 and educated at Marsden School and Victoria University. She has published two collections of short fiction, *Shallow Are the Smiles at the Supermarket* and *Animal Passions*. Her novel *Zoology* won the 1996 Montana Award for Fiction. She lives on Auckland's North Shore.

ADRIENNE KOREMAN plays in a sunny cottage within a slice of country in suburban Dunedin. She leads a busy eclectic life, juggling many projects and prospects as well as being a responsible part-time parent, student and teacher. 'Flying her own kite' is an embryonic aspiration. Her only other published work is 'Breasts' which titillates in *The Third Century*.

MAUREEN LANGFORD was born and educated in Dannevirke and now lives in Henderson Valley. She had short fiction published in the sixties, interrupted by family and work commitments, and is currently enrolled on a writing school course, with published work in a fishing magazine and *The Third Century*.

MICHAEL LAWS was born in Wairoa in 1957, and raised and educated in Wanganui before graduating from Otago University with first-class honours in history. Researcher, press secretary and then MP for Hawke's Bay (1990–96). Subsequently he wrote the bestsellers *The Demon Profession* (1998) and *Dancing with Beelzebub* (1999). He is currently completing Bill Manhire's degree in creative writing at Victoria University and writing a weekly column for the *Sunday Star-Times*.

PATRICIA LAWSON is a retired teacher of art and English living in Brighton near Dunedin. She has had a lifelong interest in writing, and has been published in *Sport* and educational magazines, as well as having stories read on Radio New Zealand and achieving success in various short story competitions.

GRAEME LAY was born in Foxton, raised in Taranaki and educated at Victoria University. Today he lives in Devonport and writes full-time. His latest books are the novel *Temptation Island*, the young adult novel, *The Wave Rider* and *The Globetrotter Guide to New Zealand*. He is also the secretary of the Sargeson Trust.

ROSS LAY was born in Wellington in 1963 and educated in various parts of the North Island, Singapore and London. He currently lives in central Auckland where he is a parent, book reviewer and school caretaker. His writing has been published sporadically since 1986. This is his third short short story.

ELISABETH LIEBERT was born in the UK in 1969. She lives in Christchurch, where her creative output includes two sons (Dorian and Alexander), assorted poetry, several short stories and a novel, *Rhapsody*. In her spare time she studies singing and Hungarian. Éljen Magyarország!

JOHN MCCRYSTAL was born in Taupo in 1966 and educated at the University of Auckland. He currently lives in Wellington, where he works as a full-time writer and accepts charitable donations.

JOY MACKENZIE was born in Hamilton in 1947. She first came to Auckland as a bewildered eighteen-year-old and, apart from two years in Indonesia, has lived there ever since. She gained an MA (Hons) from the University of Auckland as a mature student. Her recent work has appeared in *Sport*, *The Third Century* and the travel anthology *A Passion for Travel*.

FRANKIE MCMILLAN is a graduate of Victoria University's MA course in creative writing. Previous work has appeared in *Landfall*, *Sport* and *The Third Century* and on National Radio. For many years she has lived in a remote bush-clad area in Golden Bay. Recently she has discovered a liking for city life and currently works from a studio at Cranmer Centre, Christchurch.

CATHERINE MAIR co-edited the sixth issue of *Winterspin* (July 2000). In June she hosted haiku poets from as far afield as the UK and Australia who had gathered in Katikati for the opening of the Haiku Pathway. Her poems are appearing in forthcoming issues of *Takahe*, *Poetry NZ* and secondary schools anthologies.

LAURIE MANTELL was born in Pahiatua in 1916. Married to Fred, with two children, Linda and Raymond, she began writing short stories in 1945 and has published in New Zealand, England and Australia seventy-two short stories and six crime novels, from *Murder in Fancy Dress* (1979) to *Mates* (1998). She lives in Wainuiomata and is still writing.

JAN MARSH was born in Gisborne in 1951, now lives in Nelson and has two marvellous adult children. Her short stories have been published in *Broadsheet* and a lesbian anthology, and her poems in local collections by Orchard Press. She also wrote *Focus on the Family*, a nonfiction work. Formative influences include travelling overland to England in the seventies and twenty-five years as a psychologist.

JACKIE MASON was born in Christchurch in 1964 and lives in North Brighton. Her writing experience includes sixth-form journalism, a short-story course tutored by Sue McCauley and, currently, sixth-form creative writing at Hagley Community College. This is her first published work.

ROWAN MILLER was born in Auckland in 1956 and currently lives in Northland. She has no previous convictions or publications.

KELLYANA MOREY is a graduate of the Auckland University Creative writing course. Her work can be found in the first edition of this series and in the 1997 Huia Anthology of Maori writing. She is as always between residences and is writing a masters thesis on contemporary Maori art.

ISA MOYNIHAN was born in Ireland and lived in Singapore and Malaysia before settling in New Zealand. In Christchurch she is a full-time writer and fiction editor of *Takahe* literary magazine. *Sex and the Single Mayfly* won the Reed Fiction Award-and was published in 1997. A novel, *The Rashomon Factor*, will be published this year.

HELEN MULGAN was born in Hamilton pre World War II and raised on a farm. A graduate of Victoria University, she is a librarian by profession. Engulfed in motherhood for many years, she found a late vocation in writing. A supporter of Amnesty International and conservation projects, she lives in York Bay, Eastbourne.

IDOYA MUNN was born in 1974 in Madrid and grew up in Auckland. She has been writing on and off since she was a child. She studied English at Auckland University, and works in a bookshop.

BRIDGET MUSTERS lived in Europe and travelled extensively before settling in New Zealand thirteen years ago. She has been a journalist and a teacher, and her poetry and short stories have been published in various anthologies. She is a founding editor and director of Orchard Press, based in Nelson.

FRANK NERNEY, a Helensville resident, has been a journalist for many years and writes unpublished short stories and novels, reviews other people's writing, and tries to play golf in his spare time.

JAMES NORCLIFFE was born in 1946 in Greymouth, and usually lives in Christchurch, although he has worked in China and Brunei Darussalam. He has published *The Chinese Interpreter* (short stories); three collections of poetry; and several novels for children. He is currently the Robert Burns Fellow at the University of Otago.

JUDY PARKER, a former teacher and tractor driver of Greytown, is addicted to sunshine and fine writing. Previously published in *London Magazine*, *Landfall* and the *Listener*, she was winner of the 1999 *Listener* Short Story Competition. She is currently engaged in poetry and writing a novel.

BILL PAYNE learned to write in prison. Since his release he has written two books (*Staunch: inside the gangs* and *Poor Behaviour*) and won numerous awards, including the 1993 Sargeson Fellowship. Currently he is writing for film and television, recently winning a German award for his short film *Bella*, developing film scripts and reviewing films for *Southern Skies* magazine.

SARAH QUIGLEY is a novelist, short story writer, and poet. Currently based in Christchurch, she gets periodically restless. Her ideal life would be one of frequent travelling and constant writing.

SIMON REEVE is married and lives in Wellington. His work has previously appeared in *Landfall*.

ADRIENNE REWI was born in Morrinsville in 1952. She began a career in journalism in 1970, interrupted it for a twelve-year stint as a full-time artist, and now works as a full-time freelance writer based in Christchurch. She has published five nonfiction titles including the *Frommers New Zealand 2000 travel guide.*

JANE RILEY was born in Auckland in 1969. After four years living and working in Europe and Australia, she is now based in Auckland. Her career has been in public relations and more recently as publicist for TV3 and TV4. She is currently a freelance writer and PR consultant, and mother of one. As well as writing short stories, she has recently written a novel.

PIP ROBERTSON was born in Christchurch in 1977. She is a painter and writer among other things, and has a Bachelor of Fine Arts with Honours from the University of Canterbury. She is currently travelling in Asia and eating a spectacular array of fruit, the names of which she struggles to pronounce.

DENISE SAMMONS was born in Timaru in 1963. She has studied fiction writing with Owen Marshall, has had work published in *Poetry NZ* and *The Third Century* and will have a short story in an upcoming issue of *Takahe.* She currently lives in Christchurch.

VIVIENNE SHAKESPEAR was born in Auckland in 1963. She has worked in journalism, including a happy year as the *Evening Post*'s acting book page editor, and had her first short story published in *Landfall* in 1998. She lives north of Auckland with her husband and daughter.

KATHRYN SIMMONDS, twenty-seven, was born in England of a New Zealand mother and English father. Currently living in Auckland, she likes pumpkin soup, dancing and travel.

JANETTE SINCLAIR, born in Dunedin in 1948, works as a statistician in Wellington. Her novel *In Touch* was published in 1995, and short stories have appeared in *Landfall*, *Metro*, *Sport*, *Quote Unquote*, *Listener*, *Takahe* and *100 NZ Short Short Stories* (1997) and other collections.

HEATHER SNOW was born roughly twenty-six years ago in Casper, Wyoming during a blizzard (her mother claims there was no blizzard, but this is Heather's story). She grew up in Louisiana, went to university in Vermont, spent a year in Scotland, and now lives in New Zealand. 'Snow' is her first published work.

GARY P. SOMMERVILLE, born 1952, Mosgiel Otago; Suva Fiji, Titahi Bay, Suva Grammar School, Whenuapai, Victoria University, Onehunga, Asia, South America, San Francisco, Parnell, Paremoremo Jail, Massey University, Manawatu Prison, Freemans Bay, Mangonui Far North. Student, wharfie, truck driver, builder, drug dealer, jail librarian, BA graduate, fisherman, surfing dinosaur and high priest of chili.

BERNARD STEEDS is an award-winning short story writer and journalist. He lives in Wellington.

STEPHEN STRATFORD was born in Tauranga in 1953 and lives in Auckland. He is the editor of *Architecture NZ*, writes for *Urbis*, reviews for *Good Morning*, and has contributed to the

Economist and the *Spectator*. He has published fiction and nonfiction, and was convenor of judges for the 2000 Montana Book Awards.

BRONWYN TATE was born in Warkworth in 1959, and educated there and in Auckland before travelling overseas. She lives at the beach, has three children, and divides her spare time between teaching and writing. She has published numerous short stories and two novels, *Leaving for Townsville* (1997) and *Russian Dolls* (1999).

KAREN TAY was born in 1981 and is currently residing in Auckland. She has never been published before, and though she would love to share intimate details of her life, she has been discouraged from doing so because this is not a personals ad. She lives by the motto *'carpe diem'*.

JON THOMAS was born in London but has been a New Zealander since 1973. Semi-retired, he lives at Waipapakauri on Ninety Mile Beach. He was published in Tandem's first *100 New Zealand Short Short Stories* and in 1993 won the *Sunday Star* short story contest. All his life he has been writing novels, none of which are finished.

DENA THORNE-PEZET was born in 1964. She is an English lawyer who moved to New Zealand in 1997. She has had numerous nonfiction articles published and one other short story. Currently working on a book of short stories and a novel, she is moving to Melbourne soon to do a post-graduate diploma in creative writing.

JANET TYLER was born in Wellington in 1971. Since graduating from Otago University with a degree in French literature, she has worked in Auckland and London as a publicist, freelance writer, and a film and television development assistant. She is currently living in Amsterdam.

RICHARD VON STURMER is based in Rochester, upstate New York. Each year he experiences four distinct seasons: a brief spring, a humid summer, a golden autumn, and a long, cold winter. When the icicles begin to lengthen, he dreams of swimming in the Pacific Ocean.

LESLEY WALLIS began writing fiction three years ago, and her first novel *Facing the Music* was published in 1999. She is a die-hard Wellingtonian and lives in the city with her family.

GERRY WEBB was probably conceived on his parents' wedding night. He was a Commonwealth Scholar who turned off, dropped out, lived out a country dream (in the Far North) and now teaches in Auckland. He has had poems published in *Printout* and *Trout*, reviews in the *Listener*, and appeared in *Another 100 New Zealand Short Short Stories*.

SARAH WEIR won the 1999 Joan Faulkner Blake short story competition, came runner up in the *Takahe* competition and was editor's choice for Fish, an Irish competition. She has been published in the *Penguin 25 New Fiction Anthology*, *The Third Century*, *Sport* and *Takahe*. She has just completed her first novel.

JO WHITE, born 1960, is a partner in an Auckland advertising agency. She has spent her working life to date in advertising, an industry said by the cynical to be the birthplace of fiction writing. This is her second story to appear in Tandem's *NZ Short Short Stories* series.

JUDITH WHITE won the 1988 BNZ Katherine Mansfield Centenary Award for a collection of short stories and she has twice won the Auckland Star competition. Her short story collection *Visiting Ghosts* was published in 1991. She was a Frank Sargeson Fellow in 1996. *Across The Dreaming Night*, her first novel, was short-listed for the 2000 Montana Book Awards.

PHILIP WILSON was born in Lower Hutt in 1922. During World War II he served for four years as navigator/co-pilot in Ventura fighter-bombers in the Solomon Islands. Later, he attended Auckland Teachers College then worked on the *Listener*. He has published five novels and two collections of short stories, and has four children and seven grandchildren.

LOUISE WRIGHTSON is a bookseller, living in Wellington near Otari Wilton's Bush. Her short stories, prose poems and poetry have been published in *Landfall*, *Sport*, *Metro*, *Quote Unquote* and in several anthologies.